GHOSTSITTERS

ALSO BY
ANGIE SAGE

·5·
ARAMINTA SPOOKIE

GHOSTSITTERS

as told to
ANGIE SAGE

illustrated by
JIMMY PICKERING

KATHERINE TEGEN BOOKS
An Imprint of HarperCollins*Publishers*

Araminta Spookie 5: Ghostsitters

Text copyright © 2008 by Angie Sage

Illustrations copyright © 2008 by Jimmy Pickering

HarperCollins Children's Books, a division of HarperCollins
Publishers, 1350 Avenue of the Americas, New York, NY 10019.

www.harpercollinschildrens.com

Library of Congress Cataloging-in-Publication Data

Sage, Angie.

Ghostsitters / as told to Angie Sage ; illustrated by Jimmy
Pickering. — 1st ed.

p. cm. — (Araminta Spookie ; 5)

Summary: While all of the adults are away on a trip, Araminta's
cousin Mathilda comes to babysit, reluctantly bringing with her two
teenage poltergeists who proceed to wreak havoc in Spookie House.

ISBN 978-0-06-144922-2 (trade bdg.)

[1. Poltergeists—Fiction. 2. Babysitters—Fiction. 3. Ghosts—
Fiction. 4. Haunted houses—Fiction.] I. Pickering, Jimmy, ill.
II. Title.

PZ7.S13035Gho 2008   2008010434

[Fic]—dc22   CIP

                                                              AC

Typography by Amy Ryan

2 3 4 5 6 7 8 9 10

❖

First Edition

For Charlie Denchfield

CONTENTS

SLUGS

My uncle Drac says some funny things. Last week he said, "There is always a slug in the lettuce sandwich of life, Minty."

I had to think for a while until I understood what he meant. You see, Uncle Drac loves lettuce sandwiches, but even he does not like slugs. I figured he meant that just when you are enjoying something—like eating your favorite kind of sandwich—something yucky always happens (like finding a slug in it) to stop you from enjoying it.

Sometimes Uncle Drac is a little bit gloomy, so I do not always take notice of what he says—but last week I could see exactly what he meant. I kept thinking really good things were happening and then they turned out to have a great big fat slug in them.

Last Monday was the beginning of spring break, which Wanda and I had been looking forward to. And in three days' time it was going to be my birthday, which I was *really* looking forward to—although I am not sure if Wanda was.

Wanda is Wanda Wizzard, and she lives with me in Spookie House. She didn't always live here, but it is much more fun since Wanda, her mom, Brenda, and her dad, Barry, moved in. Of course there is also my uncle Drac, who can be quite fun sometimes too, and then there is my aunt Tabby, who is never fun—even though she thinks she is.

Wanda and I were eating our breakfast in the third-kitchen-on-the-left-just-past-the-boiler-room when Aunt Tabby—who was stirring the oatmeal and opening her mail at the same time—let out an excited shriek. Wanda and I both nearly jumped off our chairs, as Aunt Tabby does not usually shriek (unless Uncle Drac drops a wardrobe on her foot). In fact Aunt Tabby was so excited that she dropped the rest of the mail in the oatmeal and all the ink ran off the envelopes and turned it blue, so we were allowed to have Brenda's Choco-Drop Krackles for breakfast instead.

Aunt Tabby threw the letter on the table and squeaked, "I've *won*!"

"Won what, Aunt Tabby?" I asked.

"The competition!" said Aunt Tabby.

I was surprised, as it is Wanda's mother, Brenda, who enters tons of competitions, not Aunt Tabby.

"Drac will *love* this," said Aunt Tabby.

Although this did not exactly answer my question, it did narrow the field, as Uncle

Drac does not like many things. Basically he likes bats, the dark, and sleeping, although not necessarily in that order.

"Have you won a new sleeping bag?" I asked.

"No, Araminta," said Aunt Tabby. "It's *much* better than that."

"*Two* new sleeping bags?" said Wanda, who does not have a great imagination. "Or three new sleeping bags or maybe even *four*—"

"No, Wanda," said Aunt Tabby very patiently.

"So what *have* you won?" I asked very *im*patiently.

Aunt Tabby gave me her wouldn't-you-like-to-know look.

"Tell us, Aunt Tabby—*please*," said Wanda, who is very nosy and can't stand not knowing things.

"Here you are," said Aunt Tabby, handing Wanda the letter. "Good reading practice for you, Wanda."

I was a bit annoyed that Aunt Tabby had given the letter to Wanda, as she takes forever to read anything and it meant that I had to look over Wanda's shoulder to read it.

"Stop breathing down my neck, Araminta," moaned Wanda.

"I'm not breathing, I'm *reading*," I told her.

"You *are* breathing," said Wanda. "You are *always* breathing, Araminta. It is very annoying."

"Well, I am *so* sorry, Wanda. I will try not to in the future."

"Araminta, Wanda," said Aunt Tabby, giving us one of her looks. "*Stop* it."

So we stopped it and Wanda read the letter, which was very interesting.

Dear *Mrs. Tabitha Spookie,*

Congratulations! You are the winner of our prize competition!

You, *Mrs. Tabitha Spookie,* are the only person who answered the following question correctly:

Which of these bats does not sleep upside down?

1. a lesser long-nosed bat
2. a Mexican long-tongued bat
3. a ghost-faced bat
4. a baseball bat

The correct answer is number 4!

We are delighted to inform you that you

have won our star prize: a trip for four to explore the caves of the giant vampire bats of Transylvania!

Our Batty About Bats! limo will pick up you, *Mrs. Tabitha Spookie*, and your three lucky companions, from *Spookie House* at 6 p.m. on the tenth of this month. Please be sure to bring biteproof clothing, boots, and a sturdy umbrella.

Once again, we at Batty About Bats! offer our warmest congratulations and hope you will have a wonderful bat-spotting trip.

> Yours sincerely,
> *Reginald Noctule*

P.S. Prize taken at own risk.

I was impressed. What an amazing prize! "That is *fantastic*, Aunt Tabby," I said. "I have *always* wanted to see the giant vampire bats of Transylvania."

Aunt Tabby looked surprised. "Have you?"

"Yes! It will be *so* exciting. What a brilliant way to spend my birthday!"

Aunt Tabby looked a bit embarrassed. "I'm sorry, Araminta," she said. "I told Brenda and Barry that they could come if I won."

"Brenda and Barry!" I couldn't believe it.

Brenda and Barry didn't even like bats. Brenda always screamed when one flew at her and Barry never stopped moaning about shoveling up bat poo. It just wasn't fair. I *love* bats.

Aunt Tabby tried to explain. "Brenda showed me the competition," she said. "It was in one of her magazines. I wouldn't have seen it otherwise. So it is only fair, Araminta."

"What about my birthday?" I said.

Aunt Tabby looked a bit flummoxed. If you ask me, I think she had forgotten about my birthday. "*Well*, Araminta," she said in the extra-chirpy voice she uses when she is trying to make you not notice something. "You and Wanda will have a *lovely* time together and then we will *all* celebrate when we get home. Won't that be nice?"

No, I thought, that will not be nice.

Because when they get home it will not be my birthday anymore—it will be just another day.

And that was the first slug in my lettuce sandwich—but not the last.

Wanda was still staring at the letter. "But the tenth is *today*," she said.

Aunt Tabby let out another shriek. "*Today?* Oh, goodness, I must go and tell Drac!" And she rushed out of the kitchen.

"Araminta . . ." said Wanda in a thoughtful way.

I smiled, thinking that Wanda was going to say something nice—like how I shouldn't be upset because she had lots of exciting plans for my birthday.

"Yes?" I said.

"Pass the Choco-Drop Krackles."

I left Wanda to pig out on all the Choco-Drop Krackles, because it is not a pretty sight watching Wanda Wizzard slurping her breakfast. As I was stomping up the stairs to our Monday bedroom, I realized that things were not as bad as I had thought—in fact they were pretty good.

If Aunt Tabby, Uncle Drac, Brenda, and Barry were all going away, then Wanda and I would have Spookie House all to ourselves—apart from Sir Horace, Fang, and Edmund, of course, who are our three resident ghosts. Sir Horace is a knight who lives in a suit of armor, Fang is his faithful wolf, and Edmund is Sir Horace's weedy page. And the more I thought about it, the better it got, because I suddenly realized I could have a birthday party! I have always wanted to have a birthday party, especially with ghosts, but Aunt Tabby does not approve of birthday parties. She says, "A birthday party will make you overexcited, Araminta, and you are quite overexcited enough as it is."

I felt so excited that I went and offered to help Aunt Tabby pack. She was not at all grateful. "No thank you, Araminta," she said. "I do not want a goldfish in my cosmetic case again."

I thought that was unfair, as I was *much* younger when I had filled Aunt Tabby's cosmetic case with water and put my goldfish in it—and I would not have done that at all if Aunt Tabby had let me take the fishbowl on vacation with us.

I decided to help Uncle Drac instead. I knocked on the little red door at the end of the landing that leads into Uncle Drac's bat turret and a gloomy voice said, "Come in, Minty."

I carefully pushed open the door. "How did you know it was me?" I asked.

"No one else comes to see me," said Uncle Drac, sounding very sorry for himself.

Aunt Tabby does not like it when I go into the bat turret because, she says, it is dangerous. I suppose it is, really, but I am used to it. Uncle Drac has taken out all the floors so that his bats can fly all around the turret, and he sleeps in his old flowery sleeping bag that hangs from one of the rafters. He was sitting on a rafter next to his suitcase—which was flowery just like his sleeping bag—and his

favorite bat, Big Bat, was sitting on his hand.

"Hello, Uncle Drac," I said in a cheery-uppy kind of voice. "I bet you are really excited."

"No," said Uncle Drac.

"But you are going to see the giant bats of Transylvania," I told him. "You *love* giant bats."

"Do I?" asked Uncle Drac.

"You know you do," I told him. I crawled carefully along the rafter. "Come on, Uncle Drac," I said, "I'll help you pack."

"Sometimes, Minty," said Uncle Drac, "you remind me of Tabby."

I asked Uncle Drac what he wanted to put in his suitcase.

"Bats," said Uncle Drac.

"How many?"

"All of them," he said. "I can't leave any

behind; it would not be fair."

You would be amazed at how many bats you can squeeze into a suitcase, and I thought we had done really well, but Uncle Drac did not agree. There were still loads of bats flying around his turret. "I'll get you another suit-case," I said.

"Tabby says we are only allowed one each, and she won't have any bats in hers."

Well, that did not surprise me, given what she felt about goldfish. "Maybe Barry would let you use his?" I said.

"I already asked him," said Uncle Drac gloomily. "He said he hasn't even *got* a suit-case. Brenda needs at least two for all her stuff, so she's taking his." He sighed and looked really miserable.

It was time for some straight talking.

"Look, Uncle Drac," I said. "You know what you told me about slugs?"

Uncle Drac looked puzzled. "I don't think I need any slugs in the suitcase, Minty," he said.

"Oh, *you* know what I mean, Uncle Drac—the slugs in the lettuce sandwich of life. Well, not being able to take all your bats is the slug. And like you said, there always is one."

"So where's the lettuce sandwich?" asked Uncle Drac miserably. I sighed. Sometimes Uncle Drac is hard work. Suddenly the little red door flew open and Aunt Tabby poked her head into the bat turret. She was so excited that she did not notice me hidden behind the bulging suitcase of bats.

"Good news, Drac!" said Aunt Tabby. "Your

mother has agreed to come and look after Araminta and Wanda for the week."

I was so shocked that I nearly fell off the rafter straight down onto the bat poo far below. Uncle Drac's mother—the dreaded Great-aunt Emilene—for a *whole week*? Half an hour was bad enough. I couldn't think of anything worse. It would be *horrible*—and I could say good-bye to any birthday party plans. It was the biggest, ugliest, slimiest slug in my lettuce sandwich of life *ever*.

BATS

You would be amazed at how heavy a suitcase full of bats is. I grabbed Wanda, who was coming upstairs stuffed full of Choco-Drop Krackles, and I made her help Uncle Drac and me bring the bat suitcase downstairs. We had to be careful because we did not want to bump the bats and wake them up.

"What's in here?" asked Wanda.

I looked around to make sure that Aunt

Tabby was not lurking like she does some-times. Aunt Tabby is even more nosy than Wanda, if that is possible.

"Bats," I whispered.

"Bats?" yelled Wanda.

Aunt Tabby appeared out of nowhere—how *does* she do it? She looked at me, Wanda, and Uncle Drac very suspiciously. "What about bats?" she asked.

"We were just talking about them, Aunt Tabby. Won't it be *amazing* to see all those giant Transylvanian bats?"

Aunt Tabby did not seem that excited. She looked at her watch and said, "Hmm . . . unless your Great-aunt Emilene turns up soon we won't be seeing any giant Transylvanian bats whatsoever. She's leaving it *very* late."

"We don't need Great-aunt Emilene to

take care of us," I said. "We can take care of ourselves, can't we, Wanda?"

Wanda nodded very hard, just like the toy dog that Brenda bought Barry to put in the back window of his van.

Aunt Tabby took no notice. "Nonsense, Araminta," she said. "You and Wanda are much too young to be left alone for one night, let alone a whole week. If Great-aunt Emilene doesn't arrive, we will *not* be going."

I saw Uncle Drac suddenly look hopeful, but not for longer than about two seconds, because just then the doorbell rang. Aunt Tabby yelled, "At *last*!" and rushed off to answer it.

In Spookie House when someone rings the doorbell it gets stuck and keeps right on ringing until you open the front door and unstick it. Barry keeps saying he is going to fix it, but he hasn't yet. The doorbell makes a really terrible teeth-on-edge noise. We all dropped the suitcase and put our fingers in our ears—which was a mistake. The suitcase shot off down the stairs on its little wheels, and as Aunt Tabby threw open the door and tried to unstick the doorbell, Uncle Drac's suitcase full of bats hurtled out and rattled off down the path.

"My bats!" yelled Uncle Drac and raced after it. Luckily Aunt Tabby was having some trouble unsticking the doorbell, so she did not hear him—although I heard her scream as the suitcase shot past her.

Suddenly the noise from the doorbell stopped. Aunt Tabby was still in the doorway and I wondered why she had not let Great-aunt Emilene in. I began to feel hopeful. Maybe the sight of Great-aunt Emilene, with her double-headed dead ferret wrapped around her neck and her little beady eyes that stared right into you, had made Aunt Tabby think again and she had decided to let us stay on our own after all.

But something told me it wasn't that, because even though all I could see was Aunt Tabby's back, I could tell she was mad. I am very good at telling when Aunt Tabby is mad—I have had lots of practice. She suddenly gets prickly like a hedgehog; her hair stands up, the tips of her ears turn red, and her shoulders get a kind of pointy look to them. And right then Aunt Tabby's shoulders looked very pointy indeed.

Wanda and I crept downstairs to see what was happening.

"What do you mean, 'unavoidably delayed'?" Aunt Tabby was saying. We peered out, and instead of Great-aunt Emilene there was Perkins, who drives Great-aunt Emilene's hearse for her.

"I mean that Madam is *delayed* in an *unavoidable* fashion," said Perkins in his weird voice that sounded like he was locked deep inside a haunted vault.

I made a thumbs-up sign to Wanda and she grinned. Things were looking good.

But then Perkins—who looked even more like a skeleton than I remembered—said, "Madam has asked me to inform you that she will arrive tomorrow."

Wanda made a thumbs-down sign. I made a face.

"Tomorrow!" Aunt Tabby exploded. "That's no good. We are leaving in"—she looked at her watch—"ohmygoodnesshalfanhour."

But all Perkins said in his voice-from-the-tomb was, "I shall return with Madam tomorrow. Good day to you," and he walked away down the path. But Perkins did not know Aunt Tabby. If he had bothered to ask Wanda and me, we would have told him he would not get away that easily, but he hadn't—so he found out the hard way.

Aunt Tabby ran after Perkins like a polecat after a tiny baby bunny.

Perkins must have heard the thud of Aunt Tabby's boots rushing down the path behind him because he sped up—but he was not fast enough. Aunt Tabby scooted in front of him and stood barring the driver's door.

"*Mr.* Perkins, before you go I have an errand for you."

"I do not do errands, madam," said Perkins in his voice-from-the-tomb. "*Excuse me*, you are blocking my way."

"Indeed I am, Mr. Perkins," said Aunt Tabby. "And I shall continue to do so until you go and fetch Nurse Beryl Watkins. *She* will look after Araminta and Wanda tonight."

"Oh no!" gasped Wanda. "Not *Nurse Watkins*."

I groaned. There are not many people in the world who make Great-aunt Emilene look like a cuddly pussycat, but Nurse Watkins is one of them.

Perkins was standing his ground. "I am not

a taxi service, madam," he said sniffily. He pushed past Aunt Tabby, pulled open the driver's door, and hopped inside.

Wanda grinned. "Good old Perkins," she whispered. "He won't do it."

I shook my head; I knew better. Perkins was a novice when it came to Aunt Tabby—he hadn't won yet. I was right. In a split second Aunt Tabby had opened the back door and was sitting right behind him, in the little flip-down seat especially for people who want to sit beside the coffin. And as she slammed the door I heard her say, "Catheter Cottage, Perkins—and *fast*!"

We watched the hearse drive away, its tires squealing on the road, and we knew it would not be long until Nurse Watkins was here.

"What are we going to *doooo*?" wailed Wanda.

"Don't worry," I said. "I have an ANW Plan."

"What's an ANW Plan?" asked Wanda.

"An Anti–Nurse Watkins Plan of course."

Wanda looked impressed. "That was very fast, Araminta."

"I know," I said. "My brain is like that—I just think fast. I can't help it."

"So what *is* your ANW Plan?"

"Well, we can't stop her from coming," I told Wanda.

"I *knooow*," she wailed.

"But we *can* stop her from staying."

"Really? How?"

"I will ask Sir Horace to scare her away. I will say the secret word and he can walk around carrying his head under his arm, moaning and clanking, and Edmund can do some of his horrible singing. Even Nurse Watkins won't like that."

"You are *so* smart, Araminta."

"I know." I smiled and went to find Sir Horace. Things always look better when you have a Plan.

NURSE WATKINS

One awful hour later, Nurse Beryl Watkins was watching like a hawk as Wanda and I said good-bye to everyone. She stood at the top of the steps at the front door of Spookie House in her nurse's uniform and nearly filled up the whole doorway. Nurse Watkins is all muscle. She has legs like tree trunks and hands like a baseball pitcher's mitt. I reckon she was a professional wrestler before she got

hold of her nurse's uniform.

The Batty About Bats! limo was parked behind the hearse, which was still there. I think Aunt Tabby must have made something blow up, as there was a lot of steam coming out and Perkins was messing around under the hood muttering rude words.

Uncle Drac was helping the driver of the limo stuff his flowery bat case into the trunk. Aunt Tabby looked annoyed because Brenda and Barry had grabbed the best seats. They looked really excited. Brenda had her best pink sunglasses on and Barry was wearing a new blue bowler hat.

Brenda was saying good-bye to her cat, Pusskins. "Look after my ickle-wickle pussy-catkins, Wanda," she said in the little girly voice she uses when she talks about Pusskins, and she dropped Pusskins into Wanda's arms. Wanda staggered under the weight because the one thing that Pusskins definitely is *not* is ickle-wickle.

"Would you like me to take care of your frogs, Barry?" I asked helpfully, since Wanda does not like frogs very much.

Barry looked at me suspiciously, just like he always does when I mention his frogs. "No thank you, Araminta. Wanda is taking care of them, aren't you, Wanda?"

"Yes, Dad," said Wanda.

"*And* Pusskins," said Brenda.

"Yes, Mom," said Wanda.

At last the trunk of the car was closed and Uncle Drac got in. "Take care of my bats, Minty," he said gloomily.

"Yes, Uncle Drac."

Aunt Tabby poked her head out of the window and I wondered what she was going to tell me to take care of, but all she said was, "And do as you are *told*, Araminta."

I did not reply.

"Bye, Dad. Bye, Mom," said Wanda a bit sadly.

"Mwa, mwa!" Brenda made kissing noises out the window. "One for Pusskins and one for you," she said—then all the windows went up.

Suddenly I saw Uncle Drac banging on his window trying to make it go down again. Uncle Drac is not good with things like electric windows. Aunt Tabby looked irritated and pressed the button for him.

Uncle Drac stuck his head out of the window. "Minty, Minty," he said, beckoning me over.

"It's all right, Uncle Drac. I will remember to watch the bats. I promise."

"No, no, it's not that. Happy Birthday for Thursday, Minty," he said, and gave me a small squashy present wrapped in cute paper with spiders all over it.

For a moment I did not know what to say. And then I said, "Ooh. Oh, *thank you*, Uncle Drac."

Uncle Drac smiled his beautiful smile that shows his long pointy teeth at the edge of his mouth and said, "I'll be thinking of you." Then he managed to press the right button for once and the window zoomed back up.

The hearse moved slowly away, coughing and spluttering, and the Batty About Bats! limo followed. Wanda and I stood at the gate and waved good-bye.

The sun was setting and the road looked nice and spooky. I guessed that Uncle Drac had let a few of his bats out in order to get the suitcase into the trunk and they were fluttering around the limo as it followed the hearse. It looked like a funeral party. I could see Uncle Drac's round white face looking back at Spookie House; he waved and looked as gloomy as if he really was going to a funeral. But I figured that even he was not as gloomy and Wanda and I were just then.

"Right, girls!" barked Nurse Watkins as soon as the bat cortège had rounded the corner. "Inside. *Now!*"

It was time for the ANW Plan. Sir Horace had agreed to lurk in the dark corner beside the clock, and when I wanted him to do his haunting bit I would say the secret word. It was a really good plan, but the only trouble was . . . *he wasn't there*.

"Ahem," I coughed, "ahem, ahem, *ahem*,"

just in case he was lurking in the wrong dark corner—because Sir Horace does get confused sometimes—but there was no sign of him.

"That's a nasty cough," said Nurse Watkins. "You need some medicine for that."

I knew that Nurse Watkins's medicine would taste horrible, so I stopped coughing at once. "No thank you," I said. "I am fine now." Coughing wasn't working—I would have to try the secret word. *"Cockroach,"* I said loudly, as Sir Horace is a bit deaf.

Nurse Watkins jumped a mile. "Where?" she screamed.

But there was still no Sir Horace. *"Cockroach!"* I yelled. Wanda joined in too. *"Cockroach, cockroach!"* But still Sir Horace did not appear. Where *was* he?

We left Nurse Watkins in the hall looking

for cockroaches and went to find some cheese and onion chips and gummy bears. On the way to the basement stairs we saw the light on in Uncle Drac's broom cupboard.

I was *so* pleased. I rushed into the broom cupboard. "Uncle Drac, you're back!" I said— very quietly so that Nurse Watkins did not hear. But it wasn't Uncle Drac sitting in his old chair—it was Sir Horace. And he was reading the newspaper with his feet up, just like Uncle Drac does.

"I said the secret word but you didn't come," I told him. "That was not very good, Sir Horace. Now we probably will have Nurse Watkins here *forever*."

Sir Horace jumped. **"What?"** he said. I could see he had been so busy reading the paper that he had not heard a word I said.

Wanda, who is nosy and always wants to know why people are doing things—even boring things like reading the paper, said, "Why are you reading the paper, Sir Horace?"

Sir Horace waved the paper in the air. **"Look at this, Miss Wizzard. The dastardly FitzMaurice is knocking my castle down."**

You may not know, but a very long time ago our ghost Sir Horace lived in a castle not far away from Spookie House. There is not much of his castle left now. Recently it has been a mushroom farm and even more recently a theme park called Water Wonderland. Old Morris FitzMaurice owns it and he is not nice. He is a descendant of the really horrible Jasper FitzMaurice who stole Sir Horace's castle from him.

Wanda took the paper and looked at it. The headline said: FISH FLATTENED! and there was a picture of a bulldozer flattening a bunch of old sheds with pictures of fish on them. I would have thought that was a good thing, but Sir Horace did not.

"Let me read it," I said to Wanda and grabbed the paper.

Wanda snatched it back. "No," she snapped. "*I* will read it." And then we waited while Wanda worked out the words. "Mr. . . .

FitzMaurice pre . . . pares site for . . . auction of well-known tourist attrac . . . tion, to be sold as seaside . . . develop . . . ment site."

Wanda gave Sir Horace back his newspaper. Sir Horace looked at the picture again. **"Those foul FitzMaurices are knocking down my castle and selling it,"** he groaned.

"But there wasn't much of your castle left," I told him. "It was only a bunch of rotten old sheds."

"That is not the point, Araminta," said Wanda. "Sir Horace loves his old castle. Don't you, Sir Horace?"

Sir Horace's only reply was to groan once more and put the newspaper over his head. It was just like Uncle Drac had come back to the broom cupboard.

When we finally got down to the third-kitchen-on-the-left-just-past-the-boiler-room, Nurse Watkins was waiting for us. She made Wanda and me look for cockroaches while she boiled our dinner—disgusting parsnip and tuna soup, which would have scared off any self-respecting cockroaches anyway.

We poured our soup into Aunt Tabby's spider plant when Nurse Watkins wasn't looking, but there wasn't anything else for dinner. Nurse Watkins said it wasn't good to eat too much before going to bed, as it gave you bad dreams. But it is not eating that gives you bad dreams, it is people like Nurse Watkins.

Then Nurse Watkins said it was bedtime,

even though it was much too early. We had to remake our beds with what she called hospital corners, then fold up all our clothes and line up our shoes while she searched under the beds for cockroaches. She didn't find any but she did find a lot of dust and candy wrappers.

Wanda and I squeezed into our hospital-corner beds and Nurse Watkins said, "Lights out, girls!" She switched off the light and we listened to her sensible nurse shoes clumping all the way down through the house.

I switched on my reading-in-bed flashlight and shone it on Wanda.

Wanda stared into the light with big eyes, just like a scared rabbit. "What if she comes back up and sees the light?" she whispered.

"We'll have plenty of warning. You can

hear those hospital shoes miles away," I said. "Do you want some cheese and onion chips?"

Wanda sat up excitedly. "Ooh, yes please."

I threw Wanda a bag of chips (I always keep an emergency stock under my pillow).

Wanda was not a bit grateful. "They're all in tiny pieces," she moaned.

I was not surprised, as Nurse Watkins had thumped the pillow as if it had said something really rude. "Well, that's all I've got," I told her.

Wanda grinned. "But it's not all *I've* got," she said.

"What do you mean?"

"Ah*aaa* . . ."

I shone my flashlight right in Wanda's face just like they do in the movies when detectives are asking really important questions. I was a detective once on an important frognapping case, so I knew exactly what to do.

"Ooh, *stop it*, Araminta. That light's really bright."

I put on my creepy detective voice. "Tell me, Wanda Wizzard, *what . . . have . . . you . . . got?*"

Wanda dived under her covers and came up with a squashed-looking bag that I had seen Brenda give her before she left. Wanda waved the bag around and said, "One hundred Swedish Fish, two bars of chocolate, and a packet of popcorn!" She patted a space beside her. "Come on, Araminta," she said, "I can't eat them all on my own."

~4~

GIRLS!

We were woken the next morning by a terrible sound. *Boooooooom. Boooooooom. Boooooooom* . . .

Wanda jumped out of bed and rushed to the door. "Araminta, the house is falling down!"

I put my head under my pillow. "No it's not," I mumbled. "It's the gong."

"What's gone?" yelled Wanda. "Where?"

Booooooom. Booooooom. Booooooom . . .

I gave up trying to go back to sleep and sat up. "It's the gong," I said very patiently. "You know, that big round thing hanging up in the hall. I used to do that all the time until Aunt Tabby put it on a hook too high for me to reach."

Wanda came back and sat down on her bed. She looked really fed up. "It's Nurse Watkins, isn't it?" she said. "She's waking us up and it's only . . ." Wanda squinted at her pink fairy watch for a long time because you have to figure out which of the fairy's wings is pointing where. It is the stupidest watch I have ever seen. After a few minutes, Wanda squeaked, "It's only *six o'clock!*"

"That is why it's still dark," I said. I hugged the blankets around me. It was cold and I could see clouds of my breath on the air. We were in our Monday bedroom, which is my least favorite room. It has two iron beds and is painted a yucky pale brown with a dark brown stripe halfway up the wall—because brown is Aunt Tabby's favorite color. The beds are very old and lumpy and they squeak a lot. I always think that being in the Monday bedroom is a bit like being a poor abandoned child in an orphanage—which that morning was exactly what Wanda and I were: poor abandoned children.

Suddenly it got even more like being in an orphanage. We heard the sound of Nurse Watkins's footsteps coming up the stairs.

Wanda looked at me in a panic. "It's *her*. Don't you have a *Plan*, Araminta?"

Now, I can usually think up a Plan for anything—but thinking of a Plan when Nurse Watkins's feet are stomping toward you is tough. That is when it becomes an Emergency Plan. But I did it.

Even though Wanda has lived in Spookie House for quite a while now, I have not told her about the emergency exits in our bed-rooms. I do not tell Wanda everything, just like Uncle Drac does not tell Aunt Tabby everything. I tell her things on what Uncle Drac calls a need-to-know basis—and Wanda did not need to know about emergency exits. They would only worry her; she would want to know why we might need them.

"Of course I have a Plan," I said. "Come on, Wanda. Grab your clothes and follow me."

The emergency exit from our Monday bedroom is through a big cupboard that goes to our Tuesday bedroom. Wanda followed me into the cupboard; I closed the door and switched on my emergency flashlight. Wanda did not look very happy. "But she'll guess we're in here," she said.

"Aha," I said mysteriously. "I said follow me, didn't I? So that is what you have to do."

I pushed my way through all the old clothes that were hanging up at the back of the cupboard and the next moment I was out in the Tuesday bedroom—which is really nice. It has two big beds with curtains around them and a fluffy rug that does not have any holes in it—which is unusual for Spookie House. Wanda tripped over my old Ghost Kit and fell out of the cupboard.

"Shh!" I hissed before she could go "Ouch!" very loudly, which is what Wanda always does when she falls over.

The next part of the Emergency Plan went like clockwork. We got dressed, tiptoed past our Monday bedroom, where Nurse Watkins was calling, "Girls . . . girls?" and looking under the beds with the same expression she had when she was looking for cockroaches.

We ran downstairs at top speed.

The final part of my Emergency Plan was for Nurse Watkins to find us in the kitchen with the table laid for breakfast, cooking oatmeal, and when she came in I would ask in a bored voice if she would like some, now that she had got up *at last*. But like all Plans it did not go quite as well as planned. Because as we scooted past Uncle Drac's broom cupboard I bumped into Sir Horace and he fell over with a horrible crash. *Drat*.

And then—*double drat*—we heard the sound of nurse shoes thudding down the stairs really fast and a loud nursey voice saying, "Girls, *girls!*"

I never thought in a million years that I would actually look forward to Great-aunt Emilene arriving, but by the afternoon I couldn't wait for that hearse to drive up and rescue us from Nurse Watkins.

Wanda and I had escaped to Aunt Tabby's room while Nurse Watkins was roaming through Spookie House hunting spiders with the vacuum cleaner. Aunt Tabby's room is at the end of the big corridor upstairs. Aunt Tabby calls it her thinking room, but really it is where she goes to eat mint creams and read the paper.

Wanda is really good at finding hidden candy and she had discovered Aunt Tabby's secret stash of mint creams under a loose floorboard, which made us feel much better. The room has a cute little window that sticks out, which Uncle Drac calls an oriel window. I was sitting there, sucking the chocolate off the very last mint cream, when I saw the hearse draw up. Suddenly I wasn't so sure that I *did* want to see Great-aunt Emilene after all.

"Wanda," I said. "She's here!"

"Who?" asked Wanda, all relaxed with mint creams.

"Great-aunt Emilene."

Wanda scuttled to the window and peered over my shoulder, breathing mint-cream breath all over me. We watched Perkins—who always moves like he is walking

underwater—slowly get out of the hearse and walk around to the passenger door.

Perkins opened the door and a shiny black boot poked out. Wanda closed her eyes tight so she didn't see what happened next—and what happened next was amazing. It wasn't Great-aunt Emilene who got out of the hearse—it was Mathilda Spookie!

Mathilda Spookie is my almost-grown-up cousin and she is the coolest cousin ever. She was wearing her really amazing black coat that goes all the way down to the ground and has lots of cobwebby things stuck to it, plus her cool hat with all kinds of dead stuff on it. She stood at the gate for a moment. Then she looked up at Spookie House, and she had a little secret smile on her face. I waved like crazy but I don't think she saw me. She pushed open the gate and came clip-clopping up the path in those really great boots that she wears and rang the doorbell.

Nurse Watkins didn't hear a thing. The vacuum cleaner was making the loud screeching sound that it always does when it has swallowed too many spiders, so Wanda and I got to answer the doorbell all on our own.

I opened the door and smiled very graciously. "Hello, Mathilda," I said. "It is very nice to see you. Would you like to come in?" I could see Wanda looking a bit surprised, as I do not usually talk so politely, but just because I don't, it doesn't mean that I can't.

Mathilda was very polite too. "Thank you, Araminta," she said. "Do you mind if Ned and Jed come in too?"

I didn't mind who came into Spookie

House as long as their names didn't begin with Aunt or Nurse. "We don't mind, do we, Wanda?" I said.

"Who are Ned and Jed?" asked Wanda, peering out and blinking in the bright sun. Sometimes Wanda reminds me of one of Uncle Drac's bats.

"Yooo-hooo!" came a couple of weird voices from behind the hedge. Wanda jumped but I am used to bigger surprises than a couple of boys sticking their heads over the hedge and making silly faces.

"Yoo-hoo!" I waved back. I thought they looked like fun. This was going to be good.

Mathilda came in. She stood in the hall and gazed around dreamily. "I *love* Spookie House," she said. "I am *so* glad Grannie can't come."

"Who's Grannie?" asked Miss Nosy Bucket Wanda Wizzard. Actually I was glad she asked, as I didn't know either.

"Oh, you probably call her Great-aunt Emilene." Mathilda smiled vaguely.

"Great-aunt Emilene can't come?" I said, suddenly feeling like a huge slug had dropped out of my lettuce sandwich and someone had added a whole bag of cheese and onion chips on the side.

"She went to get her hair done yesterday and it turned bright orange." Mathilda giggled. So did we. "So she won't go *anywhere*."

"How bright?" asked Miss Nosy Bucket.

"Bright," drawled Mathilda. "Like I need *these* to look at her." She pulled out a pair of the best sunglasses *ever* and put them on.

Wanda was goggle-eyed. Mathilda looked

so cool we couldn't quite believe she was really in Spookie House at all. No one that cool *ever* comes to Spookie House. But then Mathilda spoiled it by putting her head out of the door and yelling, "Hey—Ned! Jed! Get in here—now!" She sounded just like Aunt Tabby, who is definitely *not* cool.

"Shh!" I said. But it was too late. Somewhere the vacuum cleaner droned to a halt and we heard nurse shoes stomping down the stairs. Back to reality, I thought. There was no way Nurse Watkins was going to let Mathilda stay with us for a whole week.

~5~

NED AND JED

But she did. Mathilda was not only cool—she was clever.

Wanda and I watched, totally amazed, as Mathilda talked Nurse Watkins into letting her stay. At first Nurse Watkins said that there was no way she would "*dream* of leaving the girls with a mere teenager," and she looked at Mathilda as if to say, "especially one that looks like *that*," although she didn't say it because I

don't think she dared. But a few minutes later everything had changed and it was Nurse Watkins who was asking Mathilda if she would very kindly stay and take care of us and thanking her *so* much when Mathilda agreed. It was brilliant. I made sure I listened to everything Mathilda said very carefully, as it seemed to me that this was a really good way of getting things to work out how you wanted them to—much better than making Plans that do not always go quite how you expect them to.

We waved good-bye to Nurse Watkins as she set off down the path wearing her best blue nurse's hat and cape and carrying her little black nurse's bag. As she opened the gate I wondered why she suddenly screamed and her hat flew off as if it had been caught in a gale — even though there was no wind at all. We all giggled as we watched Nurse Watkins chase her hat down the road, and every time she tried to snatch it, it seemed to see her coming and jump just out of reach. But then Mathilda whistled a really piercing whistle and yelled, "Ned! Jed! That's *enough*. Come inside *now*!" The hat stopped and waited for

Nurse Watkins to pick it up, which she did—
with an irritable swipe.

The two boys we had seen earlier appeared
at the garden gate, which suddenly flew right
off its hinges and landed on top of the hedge.
Weird. Aunt Tabby won't like *that*, I thought.
The boys sauntered up the path and suddenly
Wanda screamed, "They're *ghosts*!"

Wanda was right. The boys were wearing
dark, kind of old-fashioned clothes and when
I looked closely I could see right through
them to the patch of sunflowers that Wanda
and I had planted. And although they were
walking—not floating like Edmund does—
when I looked at their feet I could see that
they did not actually touch the ground. Wow!
Mathilda had brought two ghosts with her.
How good was *that*?

Actually, Wanda didn't think it was good at all. I was surprised because Wanda likes Sir Horace and Fang and she *really* likes Edmund, but as the ghosts strolled in through the front door, Wanda did not look happy.

"This is Ned and Jed," said Mathilda.

Ned and Jed were standing on the doormat staring just like everyone does when they first arrive in Spookie House. **"Hello, little girls,"** they said.

"We are not *little girls*," I told them. "We are Araminta Spookie and Wanda Wizzard."

Ned and Jed bowed. **"Pleased to make your acquaintance,"** they said in an old-fashioned way.

"Well, Araminta Spookie and Wanda Wizzard," said Mathilda, smiling, "aren't you going to show us around?"

Wanda and I showed Mathilda, Ned, and Jed around Spookie House. And all the time, weird stuff kept happening.

As we were walking past Uncle Drac's bat turret the little red door suddenly flew open with a bang. This was not good, as Uncle Drac's bats are always looking for a chance to escape. A huge cloud of bats flew out and Mathilda screamed, which surprised me because I would have thought she'd have liked bats. It was really hard to close the door, as the bats just kept on coming, and it wasn't until most of the bats had escaped from the turret that we could get the door shut. There were bats *everywhere*. I knew Uncle Drac would not mind at all since he would like his bats to live in Spookie House anyway—it is

Aunt Tabby who makes him keep them in the turret. But what would Aunt Tabby say?

We continued showing Mathilda, Ned, and Jed around the bat-filled house and weird things kept happening. In Aunt Tabby's bedroom all the clothes came flying out of the wardrobe and danced around the room. They looked like hundreds of Aunt Tabbys and it was really funny. But Mathilda did not think so. She yelled, "Ned and Jed, stop it!" and the clothes stopped dancing and fell down all over the place.

As we went around Spookie House more and more things happened. Moldy curtains fell on our heads, pictures fell off the wall, lampshades spun around like tops, and books flew across rooms like great big seagulls. I thought it was great but Wanda squeaked a lot.

The funniest thing of all happened when we got to the landing. Fang was sleeping on top of one of the old chests there. As we walked past, the chest raised itself up, hovered for a few seconds, then set off along the landing, heading for the stairs. Fang woke up and looked really surprised. But he looked even more surprised when the chest hurtled down the stairs like a toboggan. Fang was great—he sat up and he looked like he really enjoyed the ride. But the chest didn't do so well; it landed with a smash, split open, and a bunch of old tennis balls escaped and rolled everywhere. But Fang didn't mind. He skidded across the hall, shot straight under the monster chair by the clock, and lay there with his tongue hanging out watching the tennis balls.

The last thing we showed Mathilda, Ned,

and Jed was the ghost-in-the-bath-bathroom. We were all looking at the bath wondering whether at long last we would see the ghost-in-the-bath when a moldy sponge hit Wanda on the back of the head. She wasn't hurt, as it was only a sponge, but she got green fuzz all over her hair. I thought it was funny, but Mathilda glared at Ned and Jed, who were hanging around with their hands in their pockets. "Ned, Jed—that's *enough*," she said, annoyed. "Go away and find someone else to chuck sponges at."

I thought that was weird. I hadn't seen Ned and Jed even *touch* the sponge. As far as I could tell, the sponge had decided to throw itself at Wanda.

Ned and Jed didn't say anything. They grinned like two naughty boys who had been caught and disappeared through the bathroom paneling—which leads into the secret passage that goes to Sir Horace's secret room. I wondered what Sir Horace would think about his visitors. I hoped he wouldn't scare them too much.

Wanda hadn't said anything since the sponge hit her, but I could tell she was going to once she thought about it. Wanda is like that. She sometimes spends a long time thinking before she says something, especially if she is in a bad mood, which is different from the way I am. I say stuff straightaway—really loudly.

But Wanda didn't wait too long this time. "Ned and Jed are poltergeists, aren't they?" she said.

Mathilda nodded.

I was *so* impressed. Wanda is not nearly as dumb as she looks. I remembered what Uncle Drac told me about poltergeists. He had grown up with one in his castle. It had been very annoying—it used to throw all his sheets and blankets around, which is why he sleeps in a sleeping bag now.

"Why did you bring them?" Wanda asked Mathilda.

Mathilda looked a bit awkward, I thought. "I had to," she said. "They come everywhere with me."

"Why?" asked Wanda.

"It's a long story." Mathilda sighed.

"Tell us," Wanda and I said together. *"Please."*

Mathilda sat on the edge of the bathtub and said, "All right, then. It's a little scary, though."

"Good," I said. Wanda didn't say anything,

but she made me sit next to her on Sir Horace's treasure chest.

Mathilda began. "You know my parents run the Spookie Ghost Removal Service, don't you?" she asked.

"You mean they take people's ghosts *away*?" I was amazed that anyone would actually want to get a ghost removed from their house—although I could see that Edmund might get a bit annoying after a while. But the thought of someone taking Sir Horace and Fang away was not nice at all. I *love* having ghosts in Spookie House—it would be really awful without them.

"Yes, their job is to take ghosts away," said Mathilda. "And recently they have been really busy. Anyway, one dark and stormy night—"

"Ooh," whispered Wanda. She shuffled

up really close to me.

"One dark and stormy night," said Mathilda, "my parents were called out to a big old house in the middle of the wild, wild moors. The owners had just moved in, and the first night they were there they got no sleep at all. As soon as they had finished eating dinner all the plates flew off the table, zoomed around the room, and began chasing them. They were terrified. They were chased all around the house by the remains of their dinner for the whole night."

Wanda giggled and prodded me. "That's like you being chased by Nurse Watkins's parsnip soup," she said.

"And *you*," I told her. "It would chase you too. And it would probably catch you and gloop all over your head because you are so slow."

"I am *not*."

"Stop it," said Mathilda, "or I won't tell you any more."

So we stopped it and Mathilda carried on. "Anyway, the previous owner had thoughtfully left the number of our ghost-removal service and they called us very, *very* early the next morning.

"Mom and Dad arrived and found Ned and Jed. They had a lot of trouble removing them—in fact they had the worst trouble they had ever had. Ned and Jed threw tons of stuff at them and refused to go. Mom and Dad did all the right things that you have to do to get rid of ghosts. They found out who the ghosts were and why they were there, but still they could not get rid of them."

"So who *were* they? Why were they

there?" asked Miss Nosy Bucket.

"About a hundred years ago," said Mathilda, "Ned and Jed were pickpockets. One night they decided to go to the big house on the moor to see what they could find— just for a laugh, they said. They didn't find much. They got bored and found the kitchen. And then, because actually Ned and Jed never did have enough to eat, they stuffed themselves full of everything they could find. When they could eat no more, they had a food fight with what was left—and then they began to feel really ill. That is the last thing they remember until they woke up as ghosts—or poltergeists. They found out later that the owner of the house collected fungi and they had eaten a whole jar of poisonous toadstools."

"Eurgh!" gasped Wanda. "Toadstools. *Yuk*."

"Not nice," agreed Mathilda. "Anyway, they decided to stay at the house and have fun throwing things and generally scaring people— and they weren't about to stop for Mom and Dad either. But they stopped for *me*." Mathilda grinned.

"Wow," I said.

"Yeah. Mom and Dad called me in. And *I* removed them."

"How?" I asked.

Mathilda shrugged. "Easy. I just told them that there were much better places to hang out than there and I'd show them some if they wanted. So they came along. The only trouble is"—she sighed—"I can't get rid of them. They go everywhere with me. They are getting to be a real pain. If I don't re-home them soon they will drive me totally bonkers."

"They could come here," I said.

"No, Araminta, they could not," said Wanda. "No *way*."

Suddenly there was a loud crash downstairs. We rushed down just in time to see Ned and Jed running out of one of the secret doors in the hall, closely followed by Sir Horace.

"Knaves, scoundrels, and rapscallions!"

boomed Sir Horace. **"Do not darken my door again, else I shall take my trusty sword to you."** And he aimed some really good swipes at Ned and Jed. But Sir Horace is an old ghost and suits of armor don't move very fast. Ned and Jed dodged about, laughing.

"Ooh, missed!" said Ned—or was it Jed?

"**Missed again!**" chortled Jed—or was it Ned?

"Stop!" yelled Mathilda.

Ned and Jed stopped and Sir Horace stomped off grumpily. They began to follow him, walking in the stiff-legged way that Sir Horace walks. But I jumped in front of them and said, "If you follow Sir Horace like that you will be sorry."

"**Ooh**," they laughed. "**We are *so* scared.**"

"You will be *very* sorry," I told them sternly. And then I tried out my newest expression—Cross-eyed Giant Transylvanian Vampire Bat About to Bite.

I don't know why, but they laughed. It was extremely rude. But then Wanda did something quite unexpected.

Wanda's dad, Barry, is a magician, and she

has learned quite a few tricks from him. Wanda doesn't do them very often, but when she does they are really good.

She slipped a small bag out of her pocket and put it in her hand. Ned and Jed were so busy laughing that they did not notice. Then she went up to them and said, "Leave Sir Horace alone or else—" which got them laughing even more.

"**Or else what?**" they cackled.

"Or else *this*!" Suddenly Wanda clapped her hands together. There was a big bang and a loud flash and lots of green smoke.

Ned and Jed yelled and ran off.

"That showed them," said Wanda, dusting her hands off.

Sometimes I am glad that Wanda Wizzard is my friend.

~6~

PIZZA

When I am grown-up and I am taking care of someone younger than me because their bossy aunt will not let them be on their own, I will definitely cook them dinner. It is only fair. But Mathilda did not cook us dinner.

It was getting really late and Wanda and I were hungry. We asked Mathilda what was for dinner. She shrugged and said, "I don't

know. What *is* for dinner?"

"But you should know," said Wanda. "You're looking after us."

Mathilda looked vague and said, "We could order a pizza."

"What do you mean?" I asked. "What's a pizza? What are you going to order it to do?"

Wanda laughed. "Cook dinner," she said. And Mathilda laughed too.

I had a definite feeling I was missing some-thing here. "What's so funny?" I asked, really annoyed, as it is not nice when people laugh at what you say and you don't know why.

"A pizza is something you eat," said Wanda. "You can get someone to cook you one in a pizza shop and they bring it to you on a bike."

Now it was my turn to laugh. "Don't be stupid," I said. "Why would anyone want to cook us something and bring it here on a bike?"

"I don't know," said Wanda, "but they do. Mom and I used to order lots of pizzas before we moved here. I miss that," she said, sounding a bit sad, then she perked up and said, "Pizzas are really yummy."

So Mathilda called up the pizza place, and sure enough, about half an hour later the doorbell rang. As Wanda and I rushed to get the door we heard a loud yell and some thuds. When we opened the door there was no one there—except Ned and Jed, of *course*. And three boxes scattered down the path. And a bike racing away down Spookie Lane.

"Drat," said Mathilda—at least that's what I thought she said, although Wanda told me later that it was something much more rude.

Mathilda ran out and gathered up the boxes. "Ned, Jed," she yelled, "you *idiots*! That was our dinner."

I don't know why Wanda said pizzas were yummy, because they weren't—although Wanda said that pizzas were not usually mashed up into cold gooey sludge with bits of grit in them.

When people are taking care of you they usually do all the cleaning up and stuff like that, although obviously you have to be polite and offer to help (and hope that they say, "That's all right, you go off and play"). But we never got as far as the offering-to-help part because Mathilda didn't do any of the cleaning-up.

We had eaten our pizza/sludge in the big room at the front of the house because

Mathilda and Wanda both said that is what you did—you ate pizza and watched TV. Well, there isn't a TV at Spookie House because Aunt Tabby does not approve of them, so I lit the fire that good old Nurse Watkins had laid

in the grate. Oops—did I just say "good old Nurse Watkins"?

Wanda and I picked up all the empty pizza/sludge boxes, plus the empty root beer glasses *and* all of Mathilda's candy wrappers— as she chewed a lot of licorice and dropped the wrappers anywhere.

While we struggled out of the door with our arms full, Mathilda sat by the fire, flicking through one of the magazines she had brought with her. She unwrapped another piece of candy. "Want one?" she asked, holding the bag out dreamily, still reading her magazine. I don't like licorice and neither does Wanda. We shook our heads and staggered out with all the yucky stuff. "Missed one," Mathilda called out as we went.

"Missed what?" I asked.

"Candy wrapper. Over there."

"Pick it up yourself," muttered Wanda.

When I am almost grown-up I will most definitely *not* sit hogging the fire, reading dumb magazines and stuffing my face with licorice while someone else cleans up my soggy pizza box. Okay, so I don't like licorice anyway, but that is not the point. I would not even behave like that with Swedish Fish.

Although there are lots of kitchens in the basement of Spookie House, the one we always use now is the third-kitchen-on-the-left-just-past-the-boiler-room, as Brenda says it is foolish to keep using different kitchens like we used to before she and Barry and Wanda came to live with us. But it is a long walk along the basement corridor to get there, and by the time we did our arms were aching. I should have realized we were in for trouble when we saw Ned and Jed leaning against the door.

The third-kitchen-on-the-left-just-past-the-boiler-room looked like something had exploded in it. The kitchen was full of a huge cloud of flour and there was food *everywhere*.

"Duck!" yelled Wanda suddenly.

"Where?" I asked, wondering how a duck could possibly cause so much mess.

And then an egg hit me on the back of my

head and ran down my neck and I dropped the pizza stuff.

Another egg hit Wanda and she screamed and dropped all of her garbage, too. Not that you would have noticed, as the floor was already covered with food. There was flour everywhere and tons of broken eggs and squashed tomatoes and jelly and milk and crushed cookies and all of Brenda's packets of Choco-Drop Krackles tipped out everywhere. It was awful, but then I saw something that *really* upset me.

"My cheese and onion chips!" I yelled.

"Where?" asked Wanda, staring at the disgusting gloopy mess that covered the entire kitchen.

"Everywhere!" I can spot a crushed cheese and onion chip at a hundred feet, and it was true, they were *everywhere*. They were stuck in the jelly, floating in the squashed tomatoes, and sprinkled all over the runny egg. I was furious. And Ned and Jed were still leaning against the doorjamb grinning like it was really funny, so I told them what I thought of them. "You are horrible, horrible ghosts," I yelled. "Go away!"

"Yes, go away and *don't come back*," Wanda shouted. "Or else!"

Ned and Jed disappeared down the corridor.

"That told them," said Wanda.

It was really yucky cleaning up the kitchen and it took forever. Wanda was very grumpy. She stomped upstairs to get Mathilda to help—since it was *her* ghosts who had caused all the trouble—but Mathilda had gone up to her room and had locked herself in. Wanda said she banged on the door and rattled it like crazy but Mathilda did not answer. So we had to do all the cleaning up ourselves. It was not the fun time that I thought we were going to have with Mathilda and two ghosts.

We cleaned up the kitchen—all except for the ceiling, which we could not reach, even when I made Wanda stand on the table holding a mop. So we had to leave it covered with squirts of tomato juice, splats of egg, and strawberry jelly. I could not help but wonder what Aunt Tabby would say about it when she got home. Quite a lot, I figured. In fact there was a whole list of stuff she was going to say quite a lot about. It went like this:

Things that Aunt Tabby
Will Not Like When She Comes Home

✱ One garden gate thrown on top of the hedge
✱ One dead spider plant
✱ One house full of bats
✱ One bedroom full
  of clothes thrown
  everywhere
✱ Five smashed picture frames

- At least two dozen moldy curtains strewn around the house
- Ditto books
- Ditto flowerpots
- One smashed-up chest
- Hundreds of old tennis balls
- One kitchen ceiling covered in food

It did not look good.

We felt really tired after we had cleaned up the kitchen but there was still more stuff to do before Wanda and I could go to bed. I had to feed the boiler with the special coal mixture that Brenda gives it and empty all its ash into its boiler bucket. That took forever. Then I had to check that the bat poo hatch where Barry shovels out the bat poo was closed to prevent the bats from escaping in the night. It wasn't—so I had to shovel out a whole sack of bat poo to get it to close properly. And then I realized it didn't matter anyway, as all the bats had already escaped. Duh.

All Wanda had to do was feed Pusskins and her kittens, and she promised to help when she had finished, but she didn't come back and I just knew she was fooling around playing with the kittens so that she did not have to help with the bat poo.

Wanda said we had to wash all the egg out of our hair because it was icky—which is a baby word—but she was right, it *was* icky. But then there weren't any towels because Mathilda had left hundreds of wet towels all over the floor of *three* bathrooms. I added that to the Things that Aunt Tabby Will Not Like When She Comes Home list and I felt really grouchy and tired because by then it was nearly *one o'clock in the morning*. What would Aunt Tabby have said? And *what* would Nurse Watkins have said?

We just fell into bed and were too tired to even draw the curtains around our Tuesday bedroom beds. But just as I was going to sleep Wanda suddenly sat up and yelled, "Araminta!"

"Wharrrrrr?" I mumbled.

"I know why Mathilda came to look after us—she's got a *Plan*!"

"Whaddyou mean?"

"When she goes home she's going to leave Ned and Jed *behind*."

"Behind what?" I was so sleepy I didn't know what Wanda was talking about.

"Behind. *Here*," said Wanda impatiently.

"She's going to leave them here, *in Spookie House*. I think she has planned it all along."

I sat up and stared at Wanda. I had a horrible feeling that Wanda was right. I added Ned and Jed to my list of Things that Aunt Tabby Will Not Like When She Comes Home.

~7~
GHOST CATCH

The next morning Wanda and I held a planning meeting in the Wednesday bedroom. The Wednesday bedroom is the smallest bedroom of all. It is lined with wood and has two portholes—it looks like a ship's cabin and it is very cozy. There are two bunk beds, which are built into an alcove in the wall. I have the top bunk and Wanda has the bottom. We sat on Wanda's bed and decided to tell

Mathilda that we knew all about her Plan to leave Ned and Jed behind. "Because," I told Wanda, "if she knows that we know, then she won't dare do it."

"Won't she?" asked Wanda.

"No," I said, "she *won't*."

But we had to wait a long time to tell her because Mathilda got up really late. It was *lunchtime* when she came down—not that there *was* anything for lunch.

Mathilda looked really cool as usual. She was wearing her awesome hat—which I *love*—and her black coat with spiderwebs and lace all over it. When she walked down the stairs, her boots made clippy-cloppy noises.

Wanda and I were lying in wait at the foot of the stairs. I jumped out.

"Ooh!" Mathilda gasped. "Don't *do* that, Araminta. You gave me a scare."

Good, I thought. "Mathilda," I said, "we know what you are planning."

Mathilda looked disappointed. "You *do*?" she said.

"Yes. We know you are going to leave Ned and Jed here when you go."

I could tell that *that* had surprised her. "Oh?" she said.

"And we don't want you to," Wanda chimed in. "We want them to go too."

Mathilda fiddled with a dead mouse on her hat. "Well, they can't go just yet, can they?" she said. "Because I am going out now and they are babysitting."

"Babysitting!" I exploded. "Wanda and I are not *babies*."

"No, we are *not*," said Wanda.

Mathilda shrugged. "What*ever*," she said. "But you need someone to stay in the house while I am out shopping."

"No we don't," I said. "Anyway, they aren't someone, they are *ghosts*."

"Well, they are your ghostsitters, then," said Mathilda.

"We already have ghosts who can sit with us, thank

you, and they are much nicer ghosts," I told her.

"We could come shopping with you," said Wanda, who likes going shopping with Brenda. "Couldn't we, Araminta?"

Mathilda looked at me. "No you couldn't," she said very definitely. "Well, not Araminta, anyway."

"Why *not?*" I asked.

"Because—oh, goodness!"

Crash! Bang! Smash!

It was Ned and Jed—of course. They were at the top of the stairs playing catch, but it wasn't with a ball, it was with a great big sword—*Sir Horace's* sword. If they hadn't been ghosts it would have been a really dangerous game to play because Sir Horace keeps his sword quite sharp.

Jed threw the sword to Ned. *Clang!* Ned dropped it. Ned heaved it up and chucked it back. Jed jumped out of the way and, *crash!* it landed on the stairs—and started rolling down toward us.

"Argh!" yelled Wanda. "Get out of the way, Araminta!"

I thought Wanda was being really nice and was worried about me getting in the way of the sword and being chopped into little pieces, but what she meant was that I was in *her* way. She elbowed me to one side and ran and hid behind the clock. Mathilda followed her fast. The sword was heading straight for me but luckily I am good at skipping and I jumped right over it as it passed. It came to rest on the other side of the hall. It was then I saw that there was something attached to it—a *hand*.

Of course, it wasn't a real hand. It was Sir Horace's hand from his suit of armor. Something told me that Sir Horace would not be pleased.

I went over and picked it up. And there I was, holding Sir Horace's sword, when I heard Sir Horace boom, **"Miss Spookie! So it is true, you are in league with those scoundrels!"**

I looked up to see Sir Horace at the top of the stairs. If you asked me to draw a suit of armor looking annoyed, I would draw exactly what I saw right then. And then it began to clank downstairs toward me.

Naturally Ned and Jed had disappeared, and Wanda and Mathilda were about to do the same.

"By*eee*," said Wanda, waving as she and Mathilda headed out of the front door. "I am going to help Mathilda with the shopping."

"But, Wan*da*—"

"Be good for the ghostsitters!" said Mathilda. The door slammed and they were gone. But Sir Horace was not.

He teetered down to the foot of the stairs and sat on the bottom step with a horrible teeth-on-edge crunching noise. **"I will have my hand back, Miss Spookie,"** he said. He shook his head slowly. **"Two against one is not sporting. Not sporting at all. You can tell that to your friends."**

"What friends?" I said. Right then I didn't feel like I had any friends at all. Friends do not go out shopping together and leave their other friend all on her own with an angry ghost.

"Those two young scoundrels."

"Ned and Jed are *not* my friends, Sir Horace. No *way*!"

"Indeed? Edmund assured me they were."

Edmund—huh! I might have known. "Well, they are *not*."

"Ah. Well, then, Miss Spookie, perhaps I could trouble you to help me get my hand back on," said Sir Horace, who thinks I actually *like* putting rusty bits of metal back together again.

Sir Horace's hand was really badly dented. I unwound the fingers from his sword and carefully put the sword on the floor. I could see that his hand needed a lot of work to make it fit again. I got the small hammer that Brenda keeps for tapping loose rivets back into the boiler and started straightening the crumpled edges of Sir Horace's hand—which is, of course, just an empty metal gauntlet, really. The little finger was badly bent, but very carefully I tapped it all the way around to try and fix it. As I gave it one last tap for luck I felt something come loose. With a little plinky sound a grubby old ring tumbled out and rolled across the floor. I picked it up. "Here you are, Sir Horace," I said. "Here's your ring."

Sir Horace was not a bit pleased. He sat down on the stairs and boomed. **"No! No, it is not possible. *Noooooh* . . ."** I had never heard Sir Horace sound quite so upset—not even when he had a mouse living in his foot and Pusskins chased him all over Spookie House.

"But it's a lovely ring," I

said. And it was, even though it was really bashed around and dirty. I thought it was made of gold and it had a big square green stone in the middle. I really liked it.

"You may have that if you want it, Miss Spookie. I am sure *I* don't."

It was not the most gracious way I have ever been given an early birthday present, but since birthday presents were going to be a bit thin this year, I decided to accept it. "Thank you, Sir Horace," I said, and I put it in my pocket. I decided I would wear it on my birthday, as it was the only present I was likely to get—apart from Uncle Drac's.

I fixed Sir Horace's hand back onto his suit of armor and it fit pretty well considering what had happened to it. But Sir Horace was still not happy. **"Miss Spookie,"** he said. **"I am** an old ghost now. I want a quiet life. I have, very regretfully, made a decision."

This sounded serious.

Very carefully, Sir Horace stood up and rattled like he always does before he says something important. "I have decided that if there is any more trouble from those two rogues I will have no alternative but to go and haunt elsewhere."

I was shocked. "Where?" I gasped.

"I have an invitation to a certain Catheter Cottage."

"Catheter Cottage! But that is where Nurse Watkins lives. You can't go there!"

"Indeed, Miss Spookie, I can. Nurse Beryl Watkins mentioned when she was polishing me how well I would fit into a particular alcove in Catheter Cottage overlooking her garden. It sounded quite delightful."

"But she doesn't know you're a ghost, Sir Horace. She thinks you are just a suit of armor—like I did once. She would have a terrible shock if you turned up on her doorstep."

"**I am sure she would be very pleased, Miss Spookie,**" said Sir Horace grumpily. "**And it would be peaceful there. A well-ordered house with no nasty surprises.**"

"And no nice surprises either," I told him.

But Sir Horace bowed and said, "**My mind is made up, Miss Spookie. Any more trouble and I shall be off to a quiet alcove in Catheter Cottage.**"

I watched him lurch away, leaning on his sword. It was true, I thought, he *was* an old ghost. But he was a wonderful old ghost and I *so* didn't want him to leave Spookie House.

Sir Horace shuffled back to Uncle Drac's cupboard, where he likes to hide when he is fed up. He settled down to look at the pictures of his old castle in the paper—*again*—and I stood guard to make sure that Ned and Jed did not come anywhere near. There was no way I was going to lose our nicest ghost.

SECRETS

I was still standing guard when Wanda came back from shopping. She didn't see me as she walked past with two really big bags full of stuff.

"Whoooooo," I said in my best spooky voice. *"Whoooooo . . ."*

"Argh!" she squeaked. "Don't *do* that, Araminta!"

"Whoooooo . . . What have you got in those

baaaaaaags?" I said, flapping my arms like Edmund sometimes does.

"Nothing," said Wanda, which was obviously a lie. A *big* lie. Then she tried to change the subject. "Anyway, what are you doing there?"

"I am on guard," I told her.

"Why?"

I was about to tell her that I was stopping our best ghost from leaving *forever* when a huge crash came from the basement.

Wanda rushed off and I followed. I figured Sir Horace would be safe because at least now I knew where Ned and Jed were.

They were in the first-kitchen-on-the-right-just-before-the-laundry-room. The first-kitchen-on-the-right-just-before-the-laundry-room is where Aunt Tabby keeps stacks of plates—but not anymore. Just as we got there the door flew open with a bang and a stream of plates came flying out and hit the wall opposite. Smash, smash, smash, smash, smash, smash, smash, *smash*!

Wanda screamed and dropped the shopping bags and I am sure that I heard the crunch of cheese and onion chips getting squashed. I can hear the sound of squashed cheese and onion chips from miles away.

We took cover until the plates had stopped, then we peered around the door. Yes, you guessed it—Ned and Jed were sitting at the kitchen table, grinning, in the middle of a sea of broken plates. I added the plates to the Things that Aunt Tabby Will Not Like When She Comes Home list.

"Hello, little girls," they said. A couple of

plates zoomed out and hovered above our heads like flying saucers.

"Don't you dare!" I told them.

Very slowly, the plates flew back into the kitchen and settled down onto the last teetering stack.

"Why don't you go and haunt somewhere else?" said Wanda, furious.

"Why should we? We like it here," said Jed—or was it Ned?

"In fact we like it here so much that we have decided to stay," said Ned—or was it Jed?

"Well, in that case, you can stay in *here*," I said and I slammed the door with a bang. Inside the room there was a massive crash.

"Oops," said Wanda. "That's the rest of the plates."

"Well, at least those two ghosts didn't have

the fun of smashing them," I said, then I locked the door and left the key in the lock. "They can stay in there now," I told Wanda. "Good riddance."

"But they are *ghosts*, Araminta," said Wanda. "Ghosts can go through doors."

"They wouldn't dare," I said.

Wanda had done some weird shopping. She had bought lots of gummy bears, three tins of baked beans, some cheese, a packet of Choco-Drop Krackles, and a whole *ton* of bananas. There were only two teeny bags of cheese and onion chips plus a whole bunch of stuff that for some reason I was not allowed to see, which was very annoying. When I asked Wanda why I couldn't see it she said that Mathilda had told her that I mustn't.

Suddenly it seemed that now Wanda was Mathilda's best, *best* friend. Huh.

Wanda cooked lunch. We had sliced bananas and baked beans, which Wanda mixed up in a saucepan. It was quite nice, really. Wanda stirred some gummy bears into hers and sprinkled cheese on top. I had mine with two bags of squashed cheese and onion chips and some Choco-Drop Krackles sprinkled on top.

When we had finished I felt a bit sick, and Wanda said she did too, so we decided to go upstairs and read for a while. We crept by the first-kitchen-on-the-right-just-before-the-laundry-room. The door was still closed, which was good, but Wanda pointed out that it didn't mean that Ned and Jed were still in there. And because Wanda is Miss Nosy

Bucket, she tried the door—it was unlocked.

But Ned and Jed were still there—and Mathilda was there *too*.

"Oops, sorry," said Wanda.

"Wanda, I asked you to keep Araminta out of the way."

"Sorry, Mathilda. I didn't know you were in there," said Wanda.

"*Why* is Wanda trying to keep me out of the

way?" I asked. "That's not fair."

"Of course it's fair," said Mathilda, who I noticed was busy trying to hide a whole *flock* of shopping bags. "Now go *away*," she said, and slammed the door.

Well! I was not happy. Not one bit. You would think with my birthday coming up the next day my cousin and my so-called friend Wanda Wizzard would try to be a bit nicer.

I spent the rest of the day in our Wednesday bedroom feeling sick, and if anyone had mentioned bananas and baked beans I probably would have *been* sick. But Wanda didn't care; she disappeared to do secret stuff with Mathilda. Some *friend*.

Every now and then I looked at the ring that Sir Horace had given me and polished it a bit. I was glad that Wanda did not know I had it. If she was going to keep secrets with Mathilda, then I would keep my ring secret, *so there*. And even if I didn't get any other birthday presents—which I was pretty sure I wouldn't, considering how horrible Wanda and Mathilda were being—I didn't mind. Sir Horace's ring was special. Really special.

~9~
BIRTHDAY BOTHER

The next morning was my birthday!

Usually I wake up early on my birthday and then I have to wait a long time for my presents, but that morning I woke up really late, as I wasn't a bit excited.

Wanda was still asleep so I opened Uncle Drac's present. It was a knitted bat. At least I think that's what it was. It had a long piece of string on it so I hung it up

above Wanda and waited for her to wake up. Well, actually I didn't wait. I prodded her and hissed, "Wand*aaaaaa!*" in her ear. She sat up suddenly—like she always does when she wakes up—and the knitted bat dangled right in front of her eyes. She screamed really loudly.

I felt a bit bad about that when she gave me a birthday card and a *present*. The card was fun—it had a lot of ghosts trying to blow out birthday candles and it said GHOSTLY GREET-INGS. The present was lovely. It was a ghost maze game and I have always wanted one of those. I couldn't wait to play it and I put it in our Thursday bedroom right away. Then I remembered Sir Horace's ring that I had been keeping as a birthday present and I put it on. It fit my biggest finger. The green stone sparkled and looked lovely.

It was strange not having Aunt Tabby or Uncle Drac there on my birthday. Wanda and I crept downstairs to get some breakfast and I noticed how empty Spookie House felt. Usually Brenda is either rattling the boiler or singing her favorite song, Aunt Tabby is scuttling about finding things for people to do, and Barry is thumping sacks of bat poo around. But that morning it felt really quiet and empty—and a little bit lonely.

There was no sign of Mathilda either, and her bedroom door was still closed. We passed Ned and Jed lying feet to feet on the long bench on the landing. It is hard to tell with ghosts, but they looked like they were asleep. As we tiptoed by nothing got thrown at us so they must have been. We stepped over a smashed flowerpot and crept downstairs, through the shafts of dusty sunlight that shone between the gaps in the moth-eaten curtains, which were still drawn because Aunt Tabby was not there to open them.

As we passed the grandfather clock in the hall it struck thirteen and Wanda jumped in surprise. The clock always strikes thirteen, so it didn't mean that it was thirteen o'clock—although it nearly *was*. Both hands were pointing at twelve—which, as even Wanda knows, is midday. Midday—and we had only just got up. What would Aunt Tabby have said?

We tiptoed past Uncle Drac's cupboard—I don't know why we were tiptoeing except that that is what you do when a house is very quiet—and I could not resist a peek inside, just in case Uncle Drac had come back for my birthday. Of course he hadn't. His old black cloak was hanging up like it always does, his green string scarf was slung over another hook, and his crutches from when he broke his legs were propped up in the corner. They reminded me so much of Uncle Drac that I felt really sad. And there was no sign of Sir Horace either—just the newspaper left on the chair.

While Wanda was thumping around the kitchen fixing breakfast, I went to check on the boiler. The boiler does not like being left alone for long and I was afraid it might have gone out. It nearly had. I emptied the ash and got the fire going again with little pieces of wood and coal. Soon it was blazing away, making the hot water pipes rattle and clang like they always do. There was a funny smell coming from the kitchen so I thought breakfast was probably ready, but as I was about to go, a spooky green glow appeared in the corner of the boiler room by the ash can. It was Edmund.

Edmund was the first ghost I discovered in Spookie House and when I first saw him I was really excited—and even a little bit scared—but nowadays when I see him I get the same feeling as I do when I am out shopping with Aunt Tabby and she stops to talk to one of her friends and they both go on and *on* about all kinds of stuff. Yawn.

"**Hello, Araminta,**" said Edmund in his weedy voice.

"Oh, hello, Edmund. Must rush. Stuff to do. Bye."

I was nearly out of the boiler room when I heard a booming ghostly voice shout, "**Miss**

Spookie!" and Sir Horace lurched out of the cupboard where Brenda keeps all the boiler stuff. He was followed by Fang, who stared at me with his tongue lolling out over his big white teeth. I do like Fang, but he can be a little scary close up.

"Sir Horace! What are you doing in the cupboard?"

Sir Horace did not sound happy. "Unfortunately, Miss Spookie, I have been forced to spend the night here after an incident involving a flowerpot."

"Oh dear," I said.

"The only reason I did not leave immediately, Miss Spookie, was that I wished to say good-bye."

I was shocked. "Good-bye?"

"Indeed, Miss Spookie, I am leaving for

Catheter Cottage. Please give my regards to your aunt and uncle, and, of course, the delightful Miss Wizzard. Come, Edmund, Fang. Away!" Sir Horace swung his left leg forward, the rest of him followed, and he started clanking out of the boiler room.

"No!" I said. "Please don't go, Sir Horace. *Please*."

What a horrible birthday this was turning out to be.

"Breakfast!" yelled Wanda from the kitchen— and suddenly I had a Plan. Not a big one, it is true, but a small one with potential.

"Come and have a farewell breakfast with us, Sir Horace," I said.

For a moment I thought he was going to say no. But he bowed and said, **"A fine tradition,**

Miss Spookie. At Hernia Hall we used to have many splendid farewell breakfasts."

When Sir Horace saw what Wanda had cooked for breakfast he must have been glad that he was a ghost and didn't have to eat anything. As we came into the kitchen, Wanda was taking something out from under the grill. It looked like toast with green glue on it, although I could not be sure. "What's *that*?" I asked.

"Gummy bears on toast," said Wanda, sounding rather proud.

"Oh."

"It's all we've got," said Wanda grumpily.

Sir Horace politely left his sword at the door and sat next to me. Edmund wafted around until Wanda noticed him and said, "Ooh, hello, Edmund. Come and sit next to *me*."

Fang, who still does not realize that ghosts do not eat anything, sat beside my chair and stared up at me, hoping I would feed him.

I was going to tell Wanda that Sir Horace was leaving and we had to do something fast, but I made the mistake of taking a bite of my gummy bears on toast first. It actually tasted quite nice, but when I went to open my mouth to speak I couldn't. My teeth were stuck fast.

"Wharrrarr," I said, trying to pry my teeth apart.

"Whaaaa?" said Wanda, who was having the same trouble.

"Srrr Hrrrss *sleeving*."

"Wheerr?"

"Srrr Hrrrss sleeving!"

"Whaaarrrr?"

Sir Horace came to the rescue. "**Miss Wizzard, I believe that Miss Spookie is trying to tell you that I shall be leaving shortly and going to live in a quiet alcove in Catheter Cottage.**"

Wanda was frantically trying to pry her teeth apart with the end of her spoon. "Curthtr Crrrtge!" she spluttered. *"Nerrrr!"* Any other time I would have been rolling around on the floor laughing—but not now.

Suddenly Wanda's spoon worked. "Catheter Cottage! No! Please don't go, Sir Horace, I will miss Edmund *so* much," she said. "And I will miss you too, Sir Horace," she added rather quickly.

Suddenly I had a Plan. It was only another small one and I wasn't even sure what potential it had, but what can you expect when you have used up all your energy unsticking grilled gummy bears from your teeth?

"Sir Horace," I said. "It's my birthday."

"**Indeed? Many happy returns, Miss Spookie,**" he boomed.

"And it's an old Spookie House tradition that you must grant one wish to the daughter of the house on her birthday."

"What's a daughter of the house?" asked Wanda.

"Not what—*who*," I told her. "It's me."

"I thought it might be," said Wanda.

"**So what wish has Miss Wizzard granted you, Miss Spookie?**" Sir Horace asked with a smile in his voice.

"She promised not to ask any silly questions on my birthday. Didn't you, Wanda?"

"Did I?"

"Wand*aaaa*."

"So what wish can *I* grant for your birthday, Miss Spookie?"

Aha. Sir Horace had walked right into my Plan. I was learning a thing or two from Mathilda. "Sir Horace, my wish is that you will stay in Spookie House and not go to that

horrible old alcove—which I bet is where Nurse Watkins keeps her nurse's bag. And *that* is full of all kinds of yucky stuff—take my word for it."

I saw Wanda's jaw drop. She looked impressed, I thought.

Sir Horace did not say anything for a few moments. Then he said, **"I will stay in Spookie House but—"**

"Yaay!" We cheered and then we stopped as we realized there was a "but."

"On one condition."

"Oh," I said. I reckoned I knew what that might be. I was right.

"If those two scoundrels throw anything else at me I shall leave at once."

"Don't worry, Sir Horace," I said. "They won't throw anything else at you."

But they did.

As we helped Sir Horace up the basement stairs, one of Aunt Tabby's very best vases, complete with moldy flowers and smelly green water, landed on Sir Horace's head. The green gooey water dripped through his visor—which is the little bit that he looks out of—and ran into his armor.

"Rust!" boomed Sir Horace in a panic. *"Rust!"*

Sir Horace *hates* water getting in his armor. He clanked up the rest of the stairs at top speed and headed across the hall with Wanda, me, and Fang running after him. Sir Horace was not going on his own.

"Good-bye, Sir Rust Bucket," laughed Ned and Jed, who were sitting on the monster chair by the clock.

"Good-bye, you *horrible* ghosts," I said. "*We* are going too."

Then Wanda, Sir Horace, and I stomped and rattled out of Spookie House.

~10~

HORSE~ WITH~PEDALS

Sir Horace clanked off down the garden path and out past the gate-that-was-stuck-on-top-of-the-hedge. It was a nice sunny day, the kind of day when it is fun to be outside. However, it is not fun to be outside with your best ghost who is leaving forever—especially if he is going to live with Nurse Beryl Watkins. I sighed. I was going to have to add "best ghost gone" to the list of Things that

Aunt Tabby Will Not Like When She Comes Home.

On the other side of the hedge someone had stuck a big sign into the grass on the edge of Spookie Lane. There was an arrow on the sign pointing down the lane, and it said:

AUCTION

TODAY 6 PM

FOLLOW SIGNS TO WATER WONDERLAND

Sir Horace's old castle was being sold . . . *today*!

Suddenly I had a Big Plan—a *very* Big Plan. But first there was something very important that I had to find. And I was pretty sure I knew where it was.

"Stay there," I said to Wanda and Sir Horace. "I'll be back in a minute!"

I rushed back into Spookie House. I stuck my tongue out at Ned and Jed as I zoomed past them and then I ran upstairs as fast as I could to the ghost-in-the-bath-bathroom. I opened Sir Horace's treasure chest—okay, I know you shouldn't open other people's treasure chests without asking, but this was an emergency—and I rifled through all his dusty old papers. At the bottom of the chest I found what I was looking for—the deed to his castle! Stage one of the Big Plan completed.

In case you haven't already guessed, I will tell you what my Big Plan was. Its full title was the Big Get-Back-Sir-Horace's-Castle

Plan. It was *perfect* and it went like this: I would go to the auction for Water Wonderland—which was, of course, really Sir Horace's old castle. Wanda could come too if she wanted. I would show the auction people Sir Horace's deed, which proves that he still owns his castle. Then the auction people would make Morris FitzMaurice give Sir Horace back his castle. Sir Horace could live there instead of in Nurse Watkins's horrible alcove thingy, and Wanda and I could go and see him whenever we wanted to, and we would have all of his castle—or what was left of it—to play in.

Plus, I could cross "best ghost gone" off the list of Things that Aunt Tabby Will Not Like When She Comes Home because Aunt Tabby wouldn't even need to know that he had gone. You see, there is a secret passage from Spookie House to Sir Horace's castle and Sir Horace could easily go between the two. Sir Horace often disappears into his secret room, so Aunt Tabby wouldn't know the difference. Wanda and I could even go down the secret passage to see Sir Horace—once he had fixed its scary maze. It would be fun.

But first I had to stop Sir Horace from going to Nurse Watkins's cottage. I was sure that once he had set his pointy metal foot inside her door he would never be allowed out again. I was going to have to do some Mathilda-style talking. I took a deep breath and began. "Sir Horace," I said. "There is another birthday tradition at Spookie House."

"Oh?" Sir Horace sounded a little suspicious.

"If someone has a special Plan on their birthday, you have to help them with it."

"Really?"

"Yes. If they ask you nicely."

"Ah. And would *you* be asking me nicely to help you with a special Plan on your birthday by any chance, Miss Spookie?"

"Yes. I would."

"I thought you might be. It is strange—there are so many new birthday traditions this year in Spookie House."

"All traditions have to be new sometime, Sir Horace."

"Very true, Miss Spookie. I myself remember quite a few when they were new. So what is your Plan that you require special birthday help with?"

Now, I didn't want to tell Sir Horace my Big Plan right away in case he said no. Sir

Horace can be a bit stubborn at times. So I just said, "Before you go to Nurse Watkins I would like you to come with Wanda and me to your castle."

"Why?" asked Wanda.

"*Shhh,*" I said.

"I do not wish to see any FitzMaurices," said Sir Horace gloomily. **"Or wheelbarrows."** Not long ago Sir Horace had a bad experience at Water Wonderland when Old Morris FitzMaurice put him in a wheelbarrow and locked him in the keep.

"Wanda and I will make sure you don't see any," I told him.

"We will?" asked Wanda.

"Yes," I said. "We *will*. Let's get going."

But I could see Wanda did not think this was a good idea. "It's a long way to walk," she said.

"We can ride our bikes."

"But what about Sir Horace?"

"He can ride Barry's bike," I said. "He's about the same size."

Wanda spluttered, "Sir Horace can't ride a bike!"

"What," asked Sir Horace, **"is this bike?"**

"It's a bit like a horse," I told him. "With pedals."

"Very well, Miss Spookie," said Sir Horace. **"I shall ride the horse-with-pedals to my castle. And** *then* **to Nurse Watkins's."**

I think Sir Horace was surprised that his horse-with-pedals was more pedals than horse. Wanda wheeled Barry's bike out into Spookie Lane for him to try and Sir Horace laughed. **"Miss Wizzard, you jest,"** he boomed. **"That is no horse."**

"But these are the pedals, Sir Horace," I said. "Look."

Sir Horace did not seem impressed—but when Wanda got on the bike and whizzed up and down the lane, he was amazed. **"Aha, now I see why you are called Miss Wizzard. It is the wizardry that keeps you from falling off."**

I nearly said that it was the showing off that stopped her from falling off, but I didn't.

"No," said Wanda. "It's riding fast. That's all."

Sir Horace did not get to be a knight for nothing. He is brave. I think it must have been really scary for a ghost in armor to get on a bike, but he did. Wanda and I held the back of his saddle and we showed Sir Horace how to hold the handlebars and where to put his feet on the pedals while Edmund hovered chewing his ghostly fingernails. Fang kept running in and out of the wheels, but since he was a ghost it didn't matter, although it looked weird.

"Push the pedals, Sir Horace. Push!" we said. Sir Horace pushed and the bike began to move.

"Push harder!"

Sir Horace pushed harder and the bike wobbled forward.

"Keep going, Sir Horace!"

"Faster, Sir Horace. You have to pedal faster!"

Sir Horace pedaled faster. Soon Wanda and I were running down Spookie Lane as fast as we could.

"Go, Sir Horace, *go!*" we yelled. We let go of the saddle and he pedaled off on his own. He didn't wobble once. He zoomed off down

Spookie Lane with Fang lolloping behind him and Edmund trying to catch up. I felt really proud—we had taught Sir Horace to ride a bike.

And then Wanda said, "We never told him about the brakes."

Oops.

By the time we had run back to our bikes, gotten on them, and ridden off after Sir Horace, there was no sign of him. At the end of Spookie Lane there is a sharp bend, and as we raced around the bend we nearly rode right through Edmund, who was very stupidly standing in

the middle of the road waving his arms.

I nearly fell off my bike. "Watch *out*, Edmund," I said, annoyed. "You will get run over."

Edmund was jumping up and down like a big green soap bubble. **"The horse-with-pedals bolted,"** he wailed. **"It threw Sir Horace into a hedge!"**

We followed Edmund down the sandy track that leads off Spookie Lane and goes to the beach. Soon we came to a tall, thick hedge with a big hole in it. Fang was standing guard. Sticking out of the hole were Barry's bike and Sir Horace's feet.

Wanda and I grabbed one foot each and pulled Sir Horace out. Quite a lot of the hedge came with him—but he was still in one piece. In fact he looked a lot better than the bike. Barry's bike was not the best bike in the world and it always had a few loose parts. Now it had even more.

Sir Horace insisted on getting straight back on the bike. **"If you fall off a horse you must get right back in the saddle,"** he boomed. **"Particularly if you fall off a horse-with-pedals."**

Wanda and I showed Sir Horace how to work the brakes and then we all set off. We cycled along behind the horse-with-pedals because Sir Horace knew the way—the sandy track went past his old castle.

It was fun riding along behind Sir Horace. Fang was really excited, and even Edmund was happy because Wanda had offered him a ride on the back of her bike and he was sitting sidesaddle on the luggage carrier.

Soon we could hear the sound of seagulls

and the sea. A few minutes later we were cycling along beside a wide ditch, which Sir Horace said was his old moat. And then, as we cycled around a bend, we saw the rest of Sir Horace's castle—Hernia Hall. I was really amazed, because underneath the smashed-up mushroom sheds was a whole forest of ruins, which had been there all the time. It was true that the castle did not look so great anymore, and there was obviously quite a bit missing, but you could easily see it had been a castle.

At the sight of his old home, Sir Horace slammed on his brakes in surprise, catapulted over the handlebars, and flew into the old moat. There was a loud *thud* and he landed in pieces.

Drat.

~11~

THE RING

We picked up the pieces of Sir Horace and took them into the keep, which was a funny old round tower covered with ivy. Inside were piles of old junk. It was also very smelly because it was stuffed full of sacks of old bat poo left over from the days when it was part of the mushroom farm. Morris FitzMaurice used to buy Uncle Drac's bat poo to feed the mushrooms, but he was scared of

Uncle Drac and always bought more than he needed.

We put all the pieces of Sir Horace on the ground and then, in the beam of my emergency flashlight—which I always carry with me—Wanda and I began to put Sir Horace back together.

It was a bit scary too, as every now and then we heard Old Morris FitzMaurice and his daughter, Nosy Nora FitzMaurice, walk past, showing people around before the auction.

"Best knock this rubbish down and start again," we heard Old Morris say to someone. "I left it standing because some people actually *like* this old stuff. Could be a castle theme park, I suppose."

"Huh," said the other person. "I shall knock

it down and make a parking lot. There's money in parking lots. What's in there?"

Suddenly the rotten old door to the keep creaked open. I had switched off my flashlight just in time. Wanda and I dived behind a pile of moldy old bat poo sacks. Luckily the keep was so full of junk that Old Morris and Mr. Parking Lot did not notice the pieces of Sir Horace.

It took forever to put Sir Horace together again. By the time we had finished, the wings on Wanda's pink fairy watch looked weird. They were both almost at her little pointy pink toes. I guessed it meant that it was half past five—nearly time for the auction.

"Come on, Sir Horace, it's time to go," I told him.

Sir Horace was sitting on one of the squishy

bat poo sacks. He got up and groaned. **"Indeed, you are right, Miss Spookie. I shall make my way to Catheter Cottage."** He bowed stiffly.

"No!" I said quickly. "No, I didn't mean it was time for you to go to Catheter Cottage. I meant that it is time to go to the *auction*. It is time, Sir Horace," I said very dramatically, "to get back what rightfully belongs to you!"

"What rightfully belongs to me, Miss Spookie?" Sir Horace sounded puzzled.

This was the moment I had been waiting for—the moment when I would tell Sir Horace my Big Plan. But sometimes Plans do not happen the way you plan them. Sometimes there are things that someone has not told you, so you make your Plan without, as Uncle Drac says, having all the bat poo on the shovel.

But right then I didn't know that. I pulled out the deed from my pocket and said, "Soon it really *will* be your home, Sir Horace. Because we are going to go to the auction and we will show them *this*! It proves that all this"—I waved my arms around like they do

on airplanes when they tell you how to escape—"still belongs to *you*!"

"**If only that were true**," Sir Horace groaned.

"But it *is* true," I told him and waved the deed in front of his visor just in case he had not seen it.

Sir Horace groaned and put his head in his hands, which I found very annoying since Wanda and I had just spent a very long time putting it back on. It is a bad habit that Sir Horace has gotten into; he says it helps him think. But it doesn't help anyone else think.

"**This deed is *worthless*,**" boomed Sir Horace's head.

"No it's not," I said. "It's *your* castle. The deed says so."

"**Alas, it is not. It belongs to FitzMaurice. It**

is *his*." The head let out a horrible moan. "**He paaaaaid me for it.**"

Now I was really mad at Sir Horace. "You have been telling me lies, Sir Horace." I looked at him sternly. "That is not what you said before."

"**I only discovered the truth yesterday,**" said his head with a big sigh.

"Yesterday?" asked Wanda. "What happened yesterday?" Which was exactly the question I was going to ask.

"*I* am chief detective here, Wanda," I told her. "So I ask the questions." And before she could disagree I said, "What happened yesterday, Sir Horace?"

"**You know what happened yesterday, Miss Spookie. The ring that you are wearing. *That* happened yesterday.**"

"Yes, where *did* you get that ring, Araminta?" asked Wanda suspiciously. "What have you been doing?"

"It's nothing to do with *me*," I said, feeling like someone who suddenly realizes they are the prime suspect when they thought they had only been asked to the police station for a friendly chat over a cup of tea.

"It's always *something* to do with you," said Wanda.

"It is *not!*"

"**Stop!**" boomed Sir Horace's head, which sounded horribly like Nurse Watkins. "**I will explain.**"

So we sat in that smelly old ruin, with one of the pink fairy's wings slowly ticking its way toward her right knee and six o'clock, and we listened to the terrible story of what had happened five hundred years ago in the caves far below us.

Sir Horace put his head next to him on an old bat poo sack, then he leaned against the wall and his head began to speak.

"I shall tell you the terrible tale of how I became a ghost." His voice echoed around the keep and sounded really spooky. Wanda and I shivered and I got goose bumps all over.

"The FitzMaurices were brigands and thieves," Sir Horace began. **"They lived in a huge castle in the next valley, but that was not enough for them—they wanted my castle too. One night Fang ran off, which he often did at a full moon. Edmund and I went out looking for him and we were ambushed by a party of FitzMaurices. They were a nasty bunch, Miss Spookie. Armed to the teeth with cudgels, swords,**

pikestaffs, and fierce hunting dogs. Edmund and I fought but we were outnumbered. We escaped to the grotto beneath my castle. I was sure we would be safe there, but in our haste we sprang our own portcullis trap and trapped ourselves."

"I bet it was Edmund who sprang it," I whispered to Wanda.

"Shh!" said Wanda sharply. "That is not nice, Araminta."

"Trapped in our own grotto . . ." Sir Horace's head moaned. "I was struck down by the dastardly Jasper FitzMaurice, the leader of the gang. As I lay injured, he laughed and told his gang to pile up the rocks to stop our escape and to leave us to drown. He said my castle was *his* now. But I told him that if he took my castle he would be not only a murderer but a thief. So he took off his ring and threw it at me, saying he would *buy* my hovel—as he called it."

"Ooh," gasped Wanda. "That was *so* rude."

"**Indeed, Miss Wizzard,**" sighed the head on the bat poo sack. "**The FitzMaurices have never had any manners.**"

"So what happened *then*?" asked Wanda.

"**I threw the ring back because in those days you could offer a ring for anything.**"

"Even a rubbish old ring?" asked Wanda.

"**Yes. Its value did not matter. If you put the ring on your finger, it meant that you agreed to the deal. I told Jasper FitzMaurice that his worthless junk would not buy one brick of my castle. That is the last thing I remember. Now, Edmund—**"

Edmund jumped up and stood to attention. "**Yes, Sir Horace,**" he squeaked.

"What happened next? Tell me."

Edmund coughed. "Um . . . the big FitzMaurice, he, um, picked up the ring. He took off your gauntlet and pushed the ring onto your little finger and, um . . . he said: 'I am no thief. This is payment. The castle is mine.' "

"Ooh!" gasped Wanda. "That is *so* naughty."

"It was very naughty, Wanda," said Edmund dolefully. "Then the big FitzMaurice, he climbed up the rocks, and his men rolled the last one in place . . . and we were trapped, and after that it was really scary and the water kept coming in and, Sir Horace, you wouldn't wake up, so I stayed with you and . . ."

"Oh, Edmund, don't cry," said Wanda, trying to put her arm around him—which is not possible with a ghost. "How horrible. You were so brave."

"Thank you, Wanda," sniffed Edmund. "You are very nice."

"Edmund was brave," said Sir Horace's head. "And he was loyal. But he did not tell me about the ring."

Edmund stared at his feet like he had done something wrong—which he had. Aunt Tabby says that not telling about something is as bad as telling a lie.

"All these years I have thought I owned my own castle and I did not." Sir Horace's head let out another groan. "It is a terrible shock."

I stared at my finger. So *this* was the horrible Jasper FitzMaurice's ring? Yuck. I wasn't so sure that I liked it anymore.

Wanda was staring at my finger too. "So how come *Araminta* has the ring?" she asked, sounding a little bit jealous, I thought.

"Never mind that," I told her. "The point is that Sir Horace *does* own his castle. He never *accepted* the ring—Jasper FitzMaurice pushed it onto his finger. That is totally different. Now, excuse me, Sir Horace, Wanda and I are just going to get your castle back for you."

"Are we?" said Wanda.

"Yes, Wanda," I said, "we *are*."

Sir Horace stood up and put his head back on. **"Tonight there is a full moon,"** he said. **"Who knows what may be out there? You will not go alone, Miss Spookie."**

~12~

GHOST BATTLE

Sir Horace was right. When we crept out of the keep night had fallen and a full moon was rising. The castle ruins cast long, creepy shadows in the silvery moonlight. It was wonderful—really spooky.

"Wharooooooooooo!"

Wanda clutched my sleeve. "What was *that*?" she whispered.

"It's only Fang, silly," I said, although I have

to admit that Fang's howl did make me go all goose-bumpy.

"Wharoooooooooooo!" Fang howled again.

"Quiet, Fang!" Sir Horace told him. Fang whined and pawed the ground, but he did as he was told.

We set off through the ruins. Over by the old gatehouse we could see a big tent where the auction was going to be held. The lights in the tent shone yellow and cast long shadows of the people inside. I could tell which one was Old Morris—a tall, thin shadow with a scraggly ponytail. Nosy Nora was easy to spot too—a small, irritating shadow with two sticking-out pigtails. There were quite a few people in the tent, but I couldn't recognize anyone else.

Sir Horace's castle was a mess. Old Morris

had not cleaned up at all and there were great chunks of old mushroom sheds with horrible pictures of fish on them scattered everywhere. But as we walked through the ruins I was surprised by the amount of castle that was still there. We saw archways, corridors, old fireplaces, and even some weird little steps going down into the ground, probably to some dark, deserted dungeon. I thought it was great—it looked just like the ghost maze game that Wanda had given me. And then, for a moment, I thought it looked even more like my ghost maze game, because I was sure I saw a ghost—a girl in a long dress and pointy hat, flitting between some nearby arches.

I nudged Wanda. "Can you see that ghost?" I whispered.

Wanda didn't answer. She was looking

behind her with big, scared googly eyes. She grabbed hold of my arm and whispered, "Araminta—can you see *those* ghosts?"

Something about Wanda's expression made me not want to look—but I did. And what I saw was *really* scary. A whole bunch of ghosts was pouring up from the little steps that went into the ground. Just one look told me that they were not nice ghosts—in fact they looked extremely nasty. They wore thick leather tunics with chain mail and they were armed to the teeth with swords, sticks, daggers, and all kinds of sharp, pointy things. Some of them had huge dogs on leashes, which were leaping and snarling and showing big yellow teeth.

Fang growled a long, low growl and the fur went up on the back of his neck.

"*Sir Horace,*" I hissed. And then because Sir Horace is a bit deaf sometimes, I tapped on his suit of armor. "*Sir Horace.* Look—behind you!"

There was a grinding sound like a pepper mill as Sir Horace swiveled around. It is not often you hear a ghost gasp, because usually they are too busy making other people gasp, but Sir Horace did. "**FitzMaurice!**" he hissed. "***This* time we will win.**" He drew his sword, and to my surprise, Edmund drew his dagger. Wow. It was payback time.

The ghosts looked just like I had imagined Jasper FitzMaurice's band would look. They had gathered at the top of the steps and were swishing their swords around and waving their pointy sticks in the air. And the funny thing was they weren't making any noise. It reminded me of watching televisions in a shop window where you can see the pictures but not hear the sound—well, you can see the pictures until your grumpy aunt drags you away.

But even though they made no noise, they looked very real. They glowed a bit like Edmund but they looked very solid, like real people with real swords. The bunch of horrible ghosts gathered at the top of the steps and stared at Sir Horace. Sir Horace stared back. I held my breath. Then the biggest, nastiest ghost, who was carrying a huge ax—and was, I figured, Jasper FitzMaurice himself—took a step forward. Then all the fierce ghosts took a step forward too. And then another, and another—walking toward us very slowly and deliberately. Anyone could see that they meant trouble—big trouble.

Sir Horace stood his ground. **"So, FitzMaurice, we meet again!"** he boomed.

"We'll help you, Sir Horace," I said. "We'll show them!" Wanda grabbed my arm and tried to pull me away, but there was no way I was going to leave Sir Horace all on his own, and besides, I have always wanted to be in a ghost fight. Well, actually that is not totally true, because I never imagined there *was* such a thing. But if I had, I know I would have wanted to be in one. And there was going to be a big one any minute now.

"Take cover, Miss Spookie, Miss Wizzard!" Sir Horace boomed.

"No, Sir Horace!" I said. "We will help you."

"Don't be *silly*, Araminta," said Wanda,

jumping up and down and looking like a scared rabbit. "Sir Horace can't use his sword if you are in the way. And if he does you might get your head chopped off—and that would be awful because then *I* would have to tell Aunt Tabby."

Wanda had obviously thought everything out in great detail. But I didn't want to stop Sir Horace from using his sword, so I let her drag me away. We hid behind a wall and watched.

Sir Horace was very brave. He ran at the ghosts and swiped at them with his sword. They swiped back and jabbed at him with their pointy sticks. But of course they were only ghosts and everything went right through Sir Horace's armor without hurting him at all. But they made him twist and turn and I was not sure how well his armor would hold together. I noticed that Jasper Fitz-Maurice was standing back watching, and I wondered why. And then I realized. He was waiting for Sir Horace to get wobbly—which happened soon enough. Sir Horace's left foot swiveled around and he lurched backward. At

that moment Jasper FitzMaurice took a swipe
at Sir Horace with his ax. Sir Horace just
about managed to dodge the ax.
He swung his sword
and hit it

and I was sure I heard a *clang*.

I don't know much about ghost battles, but I do know that twenty against one is not fair. Okay, there was Edmund running around poking at people with his dagger and there was Fang biting all the horrible dogs, but even so it was not fair.

"I don't care about Sir Horace's sword," I told Wanda. "I am going to help him."

"You don't need to," she whispered. *"Look!"*

Coming out of the shadows all over the ruins of the castle were more ghosts. And they were not Jasper FitzMaurice's men—they were nice ghosts; you could tell just by looking at them. There were ladies in pointy hats and long swishing dresses, pages just like Edmund, farmers with pitchforks, cooks with saucepans and ladles—all kinds of people wearing weird old-fashioned clothes—and best of all there were *lots* of knights in ghostly armor. And they were all heading for the fight.

Soon Sir Horace had lots of ghosts at his side and Jasper FitzMaurice's men were outnumbered. Serves them right, I thought. The ghost knights swished at them with their swords; the ladies landed some good punches and one of them took off her pointy hat and used it like a sword. The farmers jabbed their pitchforks and the cooks thumped a few over the head with their saucepans and the pages ran in and out of the fight waving their knives about—just like Edmund was doing.

But Sir Horace was having a tough time because he and Jasper FitzMaurice were having a *real* fight. Every time Sir Horace's sword hit Jasper FitzMaurice's ax there was a loud *clang*. There was only one explanation for that—Jasper FitzMaurice was a poltergeist, just like Ned and Jed, and he was carrying a *real* ax. That was not good.

But Sir Horace was a really good sword fighter. Every time Jasper FitzMaurice swung his ax, Sir Horace caught it with his sword and fended it off. He got in a few jabs of his own too, but then Jasper FitzMaurice did something really mean—he aimed a hefty kick at Sir Horace's left leg. Sir Horace's foot flew off, and with an awful noise like a whole pile of tins falling over, Sir Horace crashed to the ground. Jasper FitzMaurice raised his ax up high and I just *knew* he was going to bring it right down on Sir Horace's head.

"No!" I yelled and rushed into the ghost fight.

Jasper FitzMaurice heard me and turned around. He stared at me in such a scary way that I very nearly ran right back behind the wall with Wanda, but the sight of Sir Horace lying on the ground stopped me. Jasper FitzMaurice was really tall—too tall for me to even try to grab the ax. So I did what he had just done to Sir Horace—I kicked his shin. But of course my foot went right through his leg and I very nearly toppled over just like Sir Horace.

Then Jasper FitzMaurice's ax came swinging down toward me, but before I had time to get out of the way a moldy old sack of bat poo landed right on top of him! It smelled *disgusting*, but I didn't care because Jasper FitzMaurice was lying flat out on the ground.

Then I heard Wanda yell, "Throw another one, Ned!"

"No!" I yelled. "We don't need anoth—"

Too late, another sack of bat poo came hurtling through the air and landed right beside me. It burst open and *covered* me with moldy bat poo. When I wiped the bat poo out of my eyes I saw Ned and Jed on the edge of the ghost fight, grinning as usual. But I wasn't mad and I didn't even care about being covered in bat poo. I never thought I would be pleased to see Ned and Jed, but I was. They had saved us.

At the sight of their leader laid out flat on the ground, Jasper FitzMaurice's men took off. They picked up their swords and their sharp pointy sticks, and pulling their horrible dogs behind them, they zigzagged through the ruins, then they all jumped into the moat and looked like they were swimming. *That* was weird. They clambered out on the other side and headed up the hill to where their old castle used to be. There was nothing there now but a field of pigs. I felt sorry for the pigs but I thought it would suit the FitzMaurices perfectly.

I was just thinking how well everything had turned out when someone—who sounded just like Aunt Tabby—said, "Araminta—what *are* you doing? I've been looking *everywhere*. You *know* you are not allowed out in the dark on your own. And just *look* at the mess you're in."

"Oh, hello, Mathilda," I said.

Mathilda looked very fed up. "You are coming home *right now*," she said.

"Actually, Mathilda, I am not," I told her. "Because before I come home I have a castle to return to its rightful owner."

Mathilda looked flummoxed. "You have to *what?*" she said.

So I told Mathilda my Big Plan.

I do not think it is very often that three girls (one of them covered in moldy bat poo) bring a whole troupe of ghosts, a wobbling suit of armor, and two poltergeists to an auction. I suppose that explains why everyone screamed when we marched into the auction tent. The screaming was fun—but what was even better was the expression on Old Morris's face when everyone ran out of the tent and left him sitting at the big auction table facing us all on his own.

"Hello, Mr. FitzMaurice," I said very politely. "We have come to get Sir Horace's castle back." I put the deed on the table. "It belongs to him. This proves it."

Morris FitzMaurice looked like my goldfish did when I put it in Aunt Tabby's cosmetic case. He leafed through the pages of the old deed, then he laughed and said, "Ha-ha. Very funny. This so-called owner has been dead for five hundred years. Good joke. Now go home, girls, and we'll say no more about it."

But Old Morris had not reckoned on Mathilda Spookie. "Wait a moment, Mr. FitzMaurice," she said very sweetly, fixing him with a real Aunt Tabby glare at the same time.

So Morris FitzMaurice waited a moment. And I watched as Mathilda Spookie launched into action.

~13~

SURPRISE, SURPRISE!

Wow. Mathilda had done it again! She had talked Old Morris into doing exactly what we wanted—just like she did with Nurse Watkins.

Wanda, Mathilda, and I walked back to Spookie House by moonlight. Wanda was so excited that she was gabbing nonstop: ". . . and-when-he-saw-your-ring-Araminta-that-was-*amazing*-and-then-he-said-where-did-you-get-

that-and-you-said-it's-none-of-your-business-and-he-said-yes-it-is-it-is-my-long-lost-family-heirloom-and-it-is-worth-a-fortune-and-you-said—"

"Wanda, my ears are *aching*," Mathilda complained.

But for once I was enjoying listening to Wanda because what had just happened *was* incredible. Mathilda had had a brilliant idea and it had worked. She figured the ring was worth about as much as Sir Horace's old castle. Wanda and I could hardly believe it, but Mathilda knows stuff about rings and she was right.

So when Old Morris saw his long-lost family heirloom ring on my finger I told him that I would swap it for his horrible Water Wonderland and he agreed at once! He rushed off and found the auctioneer—who was hiding in the old gatehouse—and we signed all the papers. Well, actually, Mathilda signed. She had to sign for Sir Horace because Sir Horace is officially dead and I am too young to sign anything, which is *stupid* but that is how it is. But it was me who got to give the papers to Sir Horace and tell him that his castle really did belong to him once more! That was the best moment *ever*. He rattled so much that I thought he was going to fall to pieces from shock—but he didn't. He just said, **"Thank you, Miss Spookie,"** in a husky voice and sat down very suddenly. I felt really happy.

But now, as we turned the bend in Spookie Lane and saw dark Spookie House silhouetted against the moonlight, I did not feel so great. We were going home to an empty house—a house with no ghosts. We didn't even have

Ned and Jed because they were staying with Sir Horace at the castle to keep the nasty FitzMaurice ghosts away forever.

I was also sad because I had not even had time to say good-bye to Sir Horace or any of the castle ghosts because Mathilda had suddenly become very bossy. She said something to Sir Horace and the ghosts had disappeared really fast. And now, as we walked past the gate-stuck-on-top-of-the-hedge and up the garden path to a dark Spookie House, I felt as gloomy as Uncle Drac. I was thinking that my birthday had been a very small lettuce sandwich hiding a huge, squishy slug— because in the end we had lost all our ghosts.

Spookie House was dark and quiet when we pushed open the front door. As soon as we got in Mathilda lit the big candle by the door and started whispering something in Wanda's ear. Wanda giggled and looked very excited. But I felt really miserable. It is not funny when your cousin and your so-called best friend whisper things and do not let you in on the secret—especially if it is your birthday.

Wanda and Mathilda must have realized they were being rotten because they began to sing "Happy Birthday to You" very loudly so that I would not say anything, while Wanda kept looking around with big excited eyes like a goldfish with too much fish food in her bowl.

And then the loveliest thing happened. Halfway through "Happy Birthday to You," Sir Horace walked out of the cellar door under the stairs with a huge bunch of balloons *and* Edmund and Fang. Then the most amazing thing happened—all the castle ghosts followed them!

It was wonderful. Mathilda banged the gong and yelled, "Surprise, surprise! Happy Birthday, Araminta!" and she and Wanda threw a whole storm of streamers. It was great! Wanda told me that Mathilda had arranged for all the ghosts—except for Ned and Jed, who were on guard at the castle—to rush over to Spookie House before we got home and hide in the cellar. The ghosts had to wait until they heard Wanda and Mathilda singing "Happy Birthday to You!" and then come out. I thought that was *such* a wonderful idea.

And there was even party food. That was what Wanda and Mathilda had been hiding in the first-kitchen-on-the-right-just-before-the-laundry-room—and that was why they went shopping together. We had a ton of cheese and onion chips, candies, Coke, ice cream, popcorn, Jell-O, nuts and crackers, a birthday cake with a ghost on it—and Mathilda had even made some lettuce sandwiches because she thought that I liked them. I felt a bit sad when I saw them because they reminded me of Uncle Drac, but I soon forgot when Mathilda gave me my birthday present. It was squashy like Uncle Drac's present but much bigger.

I probably broke the record for opening birthday presents. I tore off the black and red wrapping paper and pulled out the most fantastic hat I have ever seen. It was just like Mathilda's—only better! It was soft and black with tiny red spots all over the brim and black lace hanging from it like little curtains. The whole hat was drizzled with silvery spiderwebs and it was *covered* in weird things. There were silver charms, a tiny dried mouse, two dried toads, a small squashed frog, a minute lizard, and a baby bat. Mathilda said they were from her special collection and that she had decorated the hat herself—*that* was what she had been doing in her room. It was the best present *ever*. I put it on right away and I did not take my birthday hat off all night.

It was such a great birthday party. I didn't miss Uncle Drac and Aunt Tabby one tiny bit— well, maybe I missed Uncle Drac a little.

But just as we were starting another game of ghost bumps —you close your eyes and run around the room and try to bump into as many ghosts as possible—the phone rang. The phone in Spookie House has a weird, ghostly ring to it, like a bell underwater. All the castle ghosts gathered around the phone and looked at it like it was some kind of strange animal. Mathilda picked it up.

"Spookie House!" she said, still giggling at something one of the more handsome pages had said.

I could hear Aunt Tabby's voice from the other side of the hall.

"Who's *that*?" squawked the phone.

"Mathilda Spookie."

"Oh, hello, Mathilda. I would like to speak to Emilene, please, dear," said the phone.

"Um, she's not here at the moment."

"Where is she?" The voice on the phone sounded suspicious.

Well, as soon as Aunt Tabby realized that Great-aunt Emilene was not here *at all* and it was *Mathilda* who was looking after us, the squawks got so loud I reckon you could have heard them at the top of the house. Eventually Mathilda put the phone down. She looked flustered. "Aunt Tabby's coming back," she said. *"Now."*

"Now?" I gasped.

"Well, in about an hour. They are at the airport."

"At the *airport*?"

"Yes. They flew back this morning. It was all a disaster. Brenda was allergic to the bats and has developed a horrible rash. Drac got sunburned on the way to the caves and Barry was bitten on the nose by a giant bat."

I laughed, but Wanda said angrily, "That's not funny, Araminta. Poor Dad. And poor Mom."

"Is Aunt Tabby all right?" I asked.

"Oh, she's fine," said Mathilda. "I don't think anything attacked her."

It wouldn't dare, I thought.

Mathilda looked around in a panic. So did I. Spookie House looked a little different from when Aunt Tabby had left. In fact, it looked *very* different—it was a terrible mess. And the party had not helped; there were party food and streamers and burst balloons everywhere. I added "House trashed by surprise ghost party" to my list of Things that Aunt Tabby Will Not Like When She Comes Home.

"We've got to clean up," I said. "Fast!"

But before we had time to even look for a broom or a bucket or a trash bag, there was a loud ring on the doorbell. We all jumped. The doorbell got stuck as usual and kept on ringing.

"They're back!" gulped Wanda.

"It can't be them," I shouted over the ringing. "They've got a key."

"What?"

"They've got a—oh, *drat!*" The doorbell would not stop. I thought things could not get any worse, but when I opened the door to unstick the bell I realized they could. Standing on the doorstep was Nurse Watkins.

"Girls!" she gasped.

"Oh no!" I said. And then I remembered what I had learned from Mathilda and I said, "Oh, hello, Nurse Watkins. How nice to see you." And actually, I really meant it—because suddenly I had a perfect Plan.

One hour later Nurse Watkins put her mop and bucket down and said, "Finished!" And she had. I don't know how she did it, but Nurse Watkins had cleaned Spookie House from top to bottom. Mathilda, Wanda, and I had helped, but Nurse Watkins was a cleaning whirlwind compared to us. And everything on my list of Things that Aunt Tabby Will Not

Like When She Comes Home was fixed.

The castle ghosts didn't want to go, so they had hidden in the cellar again along with all the balloons and the party stuff. Wanda and I had got the bats back in the turret. Mathilda had put away Aunt Tabby's clothes. Wanda and I had put Aunt Tabby's best chest back on the landing, glued it together, and put the old tennis balls back inside. Nurse Watkins had stuck Aunt Tabby's best vase back together. Nurse Watkins had mopped the kitchen ceiling. Nurse Watkins had thrown away the dead spider plant. Nurse Watkins had swept up the smashed plates. Nurse Watkins had scrubbed the birthday cake off the rug. Nurse Watkins had swept up the cheese and onion chips off the hall floor and the popcorn off the stairs and had unwound the streamers from the clock and brushed the confetti off the monster chair. Nurse Watkins had vacuumed the Jell-O off the banisters. Nurse Watkins had wiped the ice cream off Sir Horace's visor where Mathilda had tried to feed him. Nurse Watkins had been *amazing*.

I expect you are wondering how I got Nurse Watkins to do all the cleaning. Well, Mathilda says that if you are polite to people, they are usually happy to help you. That is what Aunt Tabby says too—but the trouble is that when I am polite to Aunt Tabby, she is not happy to help me with *anything*, so I didn't believe it. But Mathilda was right and it worked with Nurse Watkins. I shall probably try it again sometime.

When I first saw Nurse Watkins at the door

I thought she was very grumpy, but then I realized that actually she was worried. She had been cycling past Spookie House and had heard the ghost party noise coming from the house. She knocked on the door to see if we were okay. When Nurse Watkins saw the mess she thought that *she* was to blame. After all, Aunt Tabby had left *her* in charge, not Mathilda. So when I was really nice and asked her to help she was *so* relieved, particularly when she heard that Aunt Tabby was coming home at any moment.

In fact we had only just put all the buckets away when we heard Aunt Tabby's key in the lock. We all quickly lined up by the door with big "Welcome Home" smiles.

Aunt Tabby ran in, then she stopped and looked really surprised. "Beryl!" she said. "So

you *are* here. Thank goodness. . . . I thought—
well, I don't know why, but when I spoke to
Mathilda I thought she was here on her own.
But how silly of me—you would *never* have
left her in charge."

We looked at Nurse Watkins and Nurse
Watkins looked at us. No one said a word.
And then Aunt Tabby screamed so loud that it
made our ears ring.

"What-is-that-you-have-got-on-your-head-
Araminta?" she yelled. "Oh-my-goodness-
there-are-dead-things-on-it!"

I smiled. My birthday hat was really creating
an impression, just like I knew it would. "It's
my birthday hat, Aunt Tabby," I said. "Isn't it
wonderful?"

"Wonderful?" gulped Aunt Tabby.
"Wonderful?"

"I think it's very nice, Minty," said Uncle Drac, walking in dragging his suitcase full of bats.

"Thank you, Uncle Drac," I said. And then I nearly screamed too, because Uncle Drac looked very weird. He was bright red and very shiny, with white circles around his eyes where I guessed Aunt Tabby had made him wear her UV light protector goggles. And he wasn't the only one who looked weird either.

Barry had a big bandage right around the middle of his face. But Brenda was the weirdest of all—she had big pink, gloopy lumps all over the parts that you could see and she had swelled up quite a lot too. She reminded me of a spotty balloon Aunt Tabby gave me for my birthday when I was little.

I rushed up to Uncle Drac and I hugged him really tight.

"Ouch!" he yelled.

"Oops, sorry. Did you have a nice time, Uncle Drac?" I asked.

"No," replied Uncle Drac.

"Oh dear," I said.

"But I am having a nice time *now*. I wanted to come home for your birthday," he said. He turned to Barry, Brenda, and Aunt Tabby. "Now, what were we going to sing? One, two, three . . ."

"No!" I said. "No, don't sing. *Please*."

"Don't be shy, Minty." Uncle Drac smiled. "Everyone has to have 'Happy Birthday to You' sung to them on their birthday."

"No. No, really I don't—"

And then they all started, including Nurse Watkins.

"Happy Birthday to you, Happy Birthday to—*ooooooh*!"

Right on cue all the ghosts poured out of the cellar door along with a whole cloud of balloons and streamers! Brenda, Barry, Nurse Watkins, and Aunt Tabby all screamed. But the ghosts from Sir Horace's castle took no notice—nothing was going to stop them from enjoying the best party in hundreds of years.

Wanda started another game of ghost bumps, and some of the knights began to dance with the ladies in pointy hats. Brenda found the birthday cake and made Aunt Tabby and Barry eat some, but Nurse Watkins did not move; she just stared and stared as though she'd never seen anything like it before in her life—which I don't suppose she had. And then a very handsome knight came over to her, bowed, and asked her to dance. Nurse Watkins stopped staring, flashed him a brilliant smile, and very elegantly glided through the hall, her nurse's cape swishing behind her as she twirled around.

"Well, well," said Uncle Drac, "a ghost birthday party. That's *wonderful*!"

"Isn't it?" I laughed. "Have a lettuce sandwich, Uncle Drac."

"Thank you, Minty," said Uncle Drac. He took a big bite. "No slugs tonight," he said with a big smile that showed his lovely pointy teeth at the corners of his mouth.

"No slugs, Uncle Drac." I laughed. "Not even a tiny one."

ANGIE SAGE, the celebrated author of the internationally bestselling Septimus Heap series, lives in a very old house in the west of England. The west of England is a `Magykal` place with marshes, ancient ports, and ruined castles. It is a great place to live and write both the Septimus Heap and the Araminta Spookie series. You can visit her online at www.septimusheap.com or www.aramintaspookiebooks.com.

JIMMY PICKERING studied animation and has worked for Hallmark, Disney, and Universal Studios. He is the illustrator of several picture books. You can visit him online at www.jimmypickering.com.

For exclusive information on your favorite authors and artists, visit www.authortracker.com.

VISIT ARAMINTA ONLINE!

Go to www.aramintaspookiebooks.com to play games,
send spookie e-cards, and learn more about the
kooky inhabitants of Spookie House.